MAX'S CAMPER

DEAD IN THE Deli

TYLER RHODES

Copyright © 2025 Tyler Rhodes

Dedicated to quiche. Oh, how we love you!

Chapter 1

"This will cost a fortune," I sighed, unable to stop grinning as I stood on the pavement on the first truly warm day of the year, eyes greedily taking in what was offered in the deli. My heart was filled with joy, my body energised like it hadn't been for months, as spring had finally sprung and the winter weather was behind me. The cold months had their own undeniable appeal, but for a vanlifer and lover of shorts and Crocs, the sight of daffodils on the country lanes as I approached this small Welsh town was enough to make me weep.

My constant companion, Anxious the Jack Russell Terrier, the smartest, most adorable dog in the county of Powys where I was currently residing barked impatiently, focus on the feast just out of reach the other side of the glass.

He pawed at the window, keening to be let loose on the baskets of freshly baked artisan bread. Sourdough, ciabatta, granary, beer-infused, and on the list went, the loaves were practically screaming at us to buy them. My eyes drifted along to the selection of quiche, pork pies, sausage rolls, tubs of olives in a dizzying array of colours, and when I caught sight of the cakes I actually had a sugar rush and went light-heated. So overpowering was the sight that it sent my taste buds into overdrive in anticipation.

Anxious by name, not by nature, scratched at my bare legs, causing me to smile as for the first time in months I was back in cut-offs and my trusty Crocs, even if the air was rather fresh.

"Yes, I think we better get inside before we collapse from excitement." I pushed on the door and the little guy raced ahead, skidding on the spotless black and white chequered floor then coming to a stop when he bumped into the floor-to-ceiling shelving containing an array of jars and bottles, olive oils, vinegars, and esoteric things like vine leaves in oil from Greece and other beauties from around Europe. But as the bell rang above the door and Anxious recovered then turned to me, we were both drawn to the left and there our feet took us without me even realising.

"Cheese!"

Anxious grinned as he studied the deli counter, and licked his lips. I did likewise. A high-pitched yip echoed around the well-stocked shop, my best buddy's impatience and hunger overwhelming him.

"Yes, we'll get lots of treats for us both. Will you look at this place? It's a chef's paradise." I couldn't take my eyes off the endless offerings the delicatessen had on display. For an ex-chef still obsessed with food, seeing so many delicious morsels was almost too much for me.

Preparing meals in my 67 VW T2 Campervan was not without its challenges, especially through the winter months when the incredibly cramped conditions had to be dealt with, so I always made it my mission to purchase plenty of groceries that needed no cooking, just eating, so this was truly paradise.

I felt at home in such places, as those who ran independent delis were always as into food as me. As with other such shops, it was obvious that the owner took immense pride in his place of business, treating each and every item with an almost religious care. The offerings like sacred relics or prized works of art, and for me, and those like me with a culinary bent, they were worthy of a pedestal in the best museum.

Anxious barked again, so I bent and scooped him up so he could get a better look at the large glass display cabinet running along the entire wall. The food was organised into sections, a sturdy divide keeping the various offerings separated. Even the trays and bowls the smaller morsels were displayed in looked nice, the overall whole like a painting it was so perfect.

Cheese ranging from traditional Cheddar, to Gorgonzola, Brie, eye-wateringly expensive local Welsh offerings, and even goats cheese were lined up neatly, screaming to be sampled. Meats sliced to paper-thin perfection were arranged in intricate spiral patterns or layered atop one another, the choice seemingly endless. Hams, brisket, pancetta, Pastrami, Parma ham, I couldn't keep up with the choices, and as I bent to study them I realised I was patting my pocket where my wallet was kept, a nervous sweat springing up on my forehead as I worried about the amount of money I would soon be spending.

We sidled along, Anxious' eyes bugging, his tongue lapping at the air and his nose twitching as he sucked and snorted in the aromas. The overriding smell was of freshness. This was no place where anything lingered for long, and judging by the numerous certificates and awards positioned on a shelf behind the counter, it was clear that people came from far and wide to spend their cash and enjoy what was on offer.

Unable to stand it any longer as my senses were becoming overloaded, I turned my back on the counter and breathed deeply and slowly, getting my over-eager chef mind under control. Anxious whined from my arms, so I rubbed his head then looked where he was pointing and almost collapsed.

On the opposite wall, set out like something from a baker's dream, was a simple shelf adorned with neat rows of cakes. Gateaux, sponge, triple layer chocolate, something super squidgy with more cream than could be legal. Even the carrot cake with a generous amount of icing adorning the heady heights, shining like snow atop an unclimbable mountain made my heart skip a beat and Anxious wriggle to get free and try his best to scoff the lot.

"You can't eat cake. You know how you get if you have sugar. You're like a little kid and start running around chasing your own tail. Then you collapse with the comedown and feel awful after your nap. It's not worth it. For you," I sniggered, licking my lips.

Anxious spun and looked into my eyes with his own mournful brown orbs, about as sad as I'd ever seen him. He'd take his chances, and suffer the consequences if allowed.

"Fine! Maybe a tiny slice of whatever isn't very sweet. I don't know what to get. I want to taste everything. What shall we have for our picnic, eh? We aren't going back to the campsite until later, as we're out for the day to have an adventure, so we need to think carefully. The fridge in Vee is tiny, which isn't ideal, so we need to pick and choose wisely."

Most of my concerns were lost on the little fella—he'd have bought the lot and not cared about the consequences, as long as he could use my bank card rather than his own—but it was just the two of us so I had to be mindful of not letting my stomach dictate my spending.

My thoughts drifted to Min, my ex-wife and best friend besides Anxious, and I lamented that she wasn't here with us. I'd spent the last few months at the campsite we'd first visited at Christmas, helping the novice owners renovate the house and finish getting things ready for the upcoming first season, and Min had visited on several occasions, our road back to once again being a couple progressing nicely.

It hadn't been without its ups and downs, both in terms of me getting itchy feet and not travelling, and pining for Min when she wasn't there, but at least we were getting closer to a time when we'd be a proper family again. We'd vowed to take a year to ensure the decision was the right one, but I already knew it was and Min had become increasingly open about how she now felt sure we'd resume our relationship properly. But she was busy with her work, had to travel to visit, and we only ever had a day or two together with us cosying up in the rock n roll bed, but no intimacy as no way did we want to push things too far too fast and cause ourselves even more grief.

All of this I understood and accepted, but the longer we were apart now I'd turned my life around and given up a stressful career and become a nomad, the more I missed her. I smiled as I thought about how excited she'd be seeing this delicious food, and wished she was here with us. Unfortunately, for the next few weeks she had a lot of work as a personal dietitian. Her clients needed her, so while she was busy helping them, I was here staring at things she tried her best to help people avoid. The irony was not lost on me, but being six one, trim, and with more muscle than I'd ever had in my life thanks to regular exercise and the work helping at the previous campsite had seemingly left me able to eat what was probably more than I should have, so the cakes beckoned and I would not refuse them. But which one, or possibly three, to pick?

I tapped my wallet again, then brushed a hand nervously through my hair. It had grown long over the course of my adventures, and I still hadn't done more than a quick DIY trim ever since I quit work over eighteen months ago now. With a tidy beard I had taken the plunge and cut, I still looked rather wild, but in at least a slightly more manicured way. Long brown locks, blue eyes, all that was missing was a tan, which always meant the sun exposure turned my eyes almost green. Weird, but true.

The bell jangled, so I turned from my cake-focused reverie to find a woman I guesstimated was approaching forty staring at me and frowning. "What are you doing?" she asked, which I found odd. She wore faded jeans with rips from use rather than pretend ageing, sensible black trainers, a green vest revealing slim, strong arms, and a crisp white apron with Del's Deli embroidered above the chest pocket. Wavy brown, collar length hair peppered with streaks of grey curtained a cherubic face with generous lips and high cheekbones. Arched eyebrows framed hazel eyes that reminded me of an anime character, as they seemed so large. A wry smile appeared to be a permanent fixture, as though she knew something amusing and insightful, but wasn't about to share.

With her hands on her hips, she held my gaze confidently, then sized me up, clearly willing to wait however long I took to answer, not needing to fill the silence.

Anxious, of course, had other ideas, mostly food based, so sidled over to her and sat, tail wagging, looking up at her with unfounded optimism. With his head cocked, he was clearly expecting not only adoration, but lashings of cake and maybe a few pork pies too.

"I'm trying to get some willpower and refrain from buying everything in the deli. I assume you work here? Come to think of it, I haven't seen anyone yet. And with this amount of food, I'd expect it to be busy."

"What's your game? Are you on the level? How did you get in here?"

Confused by her tone, and curt, snappy words, I answered, "Through the door, same as you. I'm not sure I'm following."

"Mate, it's just gone eight in the morning."

"Is it? Wow, I thought it was later. Sorry, I was up early and didn't think to check the time. I'm kind of living by the daylight and was up, so came into town and saw the deli. It's alright, isn't it? I'm assuming you've been up for hours getting the food ready and presented so amazingly?"

"I don't do that! Del does it. He's a man obsessed with food." She stepped closer, almost flattening Anxious who scooted back, tail still wagging in hope as he quickly glanced at the cakes, then she jabbed a finger at me and added, "The door was unlocked? You just walked in? Where's Del?"

"He's the owner?"

"Of course!"

"I have no idea. I saw the display, we came in, and we've been deciding what to buy. Aren't you open yet?"

"We open at nine sharp, not a minute earlier, and Del doesn't unlock until then. I start at eight to help finish getting things ready, but he's usually done it all anyway, as he's always up so early. Silly old sod goes to bed at like eight every night and gets up at four or five. He thinks he's on Breakfast TV or an early morning DJ, the hours he keeps." She glanced past me to a door behind the counter that I assumed led to the back of the building and hollered, "Del! What are you doing? Didn't you hear the bell?" When nobody answered, she muttered, shook her head, then finally acknowledged Anxious who was close to losing it by now.

"He's desperate for cake. Or a sausage roll. Or cheese. We love cheese."

"Doesn't everyone?"

"I'm Max, by the way. The food pit is Anxious."

The woman's features softened as she squatted. "Aw, the poor thing. What's the matter, my love?"

"It's his name, not his emotional state. All he's feeling right now is hungry."

Anxious was playing a long game, so lifted his paw and whined as he glanced first at the woman then the cakes.

"Is he lame? What's he done?"

"He hurt his paw last year. It worked for sympathy, so every now and then he tries it on again. Don't fall for it."

"I'm Melody," she chuckled, although I think she was addressing Anxious, not me. "What can I do to make it better, little darling?" she asked him. "A sample of sausage?" Without waiting for an answer, she jumped up, took a plate from the deli counter with tiny pieces already sliced, and bent to Anxious then let him inhale a few.

Anxious lifted his head when the sausage train stopped and raised his paw again.

"Melody won't fall for that again," I laughed, shaking my head.

"I might," she giggled, then offered Anxious another treat. "Wait here while I get Del. I don't know what he was thinking." Melody slipped behind the counter, muttering to herself about Del being incompetent and that they could have been burgled. I whiled away the time by making a mental list of what I'd buy, what I'd have for lunch, and what I'd cook that evening after a visit to the butchers next. This was going to be an awesome outing, and now I knew how early it was, I felt even more optimistic about things as we literally had the entire day ahead of us.

Melody returned looking sombre and shaking her head. She held an envelope in one hand and was so intent on it that she bumped into the corner of the door frame before looking up, coming out into the shop, then stopping in front of me. She lifted her eyes and looked at me for an unnerving amount of time, then shrugged and held out her hand. "It's for you."

"Me? What is it?"

"No idea, but you said your name was Max. That's who it's addressed to." Suddenly, she snatched her hand back and asked, "What's your surname and address?"

Confused, I told her, "Max Effort, of no fixed abode. I live in a VW called Vee, registration MAX M1N. That's my ex-wife's name."

"Her name has a number in it? Mate, that's super weird, if you don't mind me saying."

"Um, no, but that was the best custom number plate I could find. I'm hoping she'll join me in a few months. What's this about?"

"I have no idea. The envelope was on Del's desk in his little office where he likes to hide out sometimes and vape while he reads his books. It's addressed to you. See." This time she didn't snatch the envelope back and I read it in shock.

It truly was addressed to Max Effort, VW named Vee, registration MAX M1N.

"I don't get it," I said, taking it from her. "Is this Del's handwriting?"

"Sure is. I assume you know him?"

"Not as far as I know. I don't think I've ever met anyone called Del."

"Then you better open it, as he sure seems to know you."

The envelope wasn't stuck down very well, so I unsealed it then pulled out a single piece of thick paper, the off-white kind that is expensive. Melody leaned in close, Anxious brushed against my legs, and I read the words aloud. "Max, please solve my murder. Tell Melody I'm sorry about the quiche. It has a soggy bottom, and nobody likes a soggy bottom. p.s. I'm out the back by the bins. Can you make sure the coppers return the knife? It's expensive."

"Very amusing," snapped Melody. "I don't need this nonsense. You and Del might think this is funny, but I don't. Old buddies, I suppose?"

"Honestly, I don't know the man. I just wanted to buy some cheese." Anxious barked, so I nodded then added, "And cake. And meat. And pork pies. I'll skip the quiche, though, as Del is right and nobody likes a soggy bottom. He needs to pre-bake the base."

"He always does! You aren't winding me up?"

"No."

Our eyes inevitably drifted to the back room door, then Melody said, "Then we better go and check by the bins. I don't know what you two are playing at, but I don't think it's funny."

Too stunned to think straight, but as sure as Melody that this was a joke, but at my expense, not hers, I followed as she grumbled her way through the open door with Anxious hot on my heels.

We went down a corridor with the office on the right, stairs leading up on the left, then past several more rooms to a back door that was locked with an expensive padlock from the inside. Melody used a key from a large group of them, flung the door open, and stepped outside.

Her scream made me hurry for the last few steps. I found her weeping into her hands as she stood next to a large, green commercial bin. A man lay at her feet, a very expensive Shapiro knife sticking out of his throat. A pool of blood circled his head like he'd dropped a bottle of jam.

"Who are you?" gasped Melody as her head snapped around.

"I'm Max, and it looks like we have a murder to solve."

Chapter 2

"No, this can't be real." Melody shook her head, her hair standing on end from static, which I couldn't figure out.

"I'm afraid it is." I took a step towards her and placed my hand on her shoulder, feeling the bone, and frowned in sympathy.

"Get away from me!" She shook me off and shifted to the side, eyes roaming from me to Del then back again. "Who are you? What did you do? Why did you kill him? Am I next?" She was ready to bolt, and I didn't blame her, but as she tensed, her fists bunched, eyes wide as saucers, Anxious yipped.

"He's trying to tell us something. Please, don't be afraid. I would never, ever do anything to hurt you or anyone else. Give me thirty seconds to show you I'm on the level. I'm the good guy. I swear."

"Why should I trust you? You somehow get into the shop an hour before we open, you make me go and find that ridiculous note, and now you're going to murder me like you did poor Del. Why? He was a good man. The best. Hardworking, kind, paid me well, and always treated me with respect. I've been working for him for almost twenty years and we never had a cross word. He was a true diamond."

"I promise you I didn't do it. I'm going to get my phone from my pocket and show you something. If you still believe I killed Del after that, I won't try to change your mind. That okay?"

Anxious sat before Melody and wagged, then barked a word of encouragement.

Her eyes focused on him, coming back to the reality of the situation, and she nodded mutely.

With my fingers shaking slightly, I pulled out my phone, as no matter how many times I saw a corpse it always unnerved me no end. The reality simply didn't compute. People were meant to move, not be so still, and without that spark of life it made them seem like dolls, not real human beings. Maybe this was why I could cope with it, because my mind refused to accept the fact they were recently a person with hopes, dreams, worries, lovers, friends, family, and a whole existence that was now gone.

"What's with you?" asked Melody, frowning.

"Sorry, I was just thinking about poor Del. Here, let me show you this." I tapped the bookmark on my phone, then held it out.

"This might be a trap." Melody once again switched her gaze to Del, then back to me, before sighing and coming to a decision. "Don't make me regret this, Max. If that really is your name."

"Just check the phone, please." As Melody snatched the phone then stepped away, presumably in case I attacked, I suddenly felt self-conscious so teased my hair behind my ears, the length now almost too long. Maybe a March trim was in order, to celebrate the advent of spring. With my thick, albeit more controlled beard, and what Min called smouldering blue eyes, I knew that at six one I could sometimes look rather intimidating, but I never tried to use my size to make people feel uncomfortable. Years with Min at her less fearsome five five had meant I often found myself bending at the knee anyway.

"It's you on the wiki page."

"My dad keeps it updated with the murder mysteries I've helped solve. I know the photo is cheesy, he found one before my hair was so long, but see, it's me." I smiled, then mussed with my hair again, and tried not to look like a homicidal maniac. I wasn't sure I was succeeding.

"You solved all those crimes?"

"I did. It began when I became a vanlifer last summer, and I've had the opportunity to help figure out quite a few cases since then."

"Nothing for a while though. At Christmas!? You solved a murder on Christmas Day?"

"Unfortunately, yes. A terrible business. The corpse was hidden in a snowman and we found him on Christmas morning. We hadn't even had a mince pie."

"What a downer. Not about the mince pies, about the dead guy. But it says here you had snow, and that your mum and dad were invaluable in helping solve the case, along with a woman named Min, who's your ex-wife but adorable and you were an idiot for behaving so badly that she divorced you?" Melody smiled, her jaw relaxing, and she'd moved closer without even realising.

"Dad, er, likes to give away more detail than he should. He's not big on keeping things private. But don't worry about that. The main thing is that I'm not going to hurt you. For whatever reason, ever since I decided to live in my campervan, I've been embroiled in plenty of murder mysteries. Melody, the only thing I can think of that goes any way towards explaining any of this is that Del found out about me. How he knew I would be here at this specific time is beyond me right now, but I promise you that if I can, I'll help figure this out."

"This makes no sense. None." She rubbed at her forehead until she left a red mark, then scratched at her scalp, still undecided. "How could Del possibly know you'd be here at this time? How did he know he would be killed? He wrote a note! He wanted you to solve this, and even knew what knife would be used. No, I'm not having it! This is a trick. A game of some sort. Del! Del, are you even dead?" She kicked at the corpse, unable to accept he was gone, then shook her head when he didn't stir.

"Melody, don't. Please calm down. Del has passed, and in a terrible way, and I promise you this is not a game."

"You guys are winding me up. You have to be. He can't be dead. I bet it's a fake knife. I bet it's one of those retractable plastic things. A prop from a movie or something." Before I could stop her, Melody squatted, then yanked on the Shapiro knife with both hands, the expensive long blade freeing as though from a block of butter. The steel glistened as the March sun angled between buildings, lighting up the scene. Blood sparkled as it dripped from the tip.

Melody gasped, then fell back onto her bum. She released the knife and it clattered to the rough ground beside her. "It's real? He's really dead?"

"He is. You shouldn't have touched the knife. It's evidence. I know it's hard, but he's gone. Come on, we need to call the police and lock the shop door. We don't want anyone coming inside."

"But he can't be dead. It's Monday, our busiest day. We do amazing business today, and what about all the food? It will go to waste. Del wouldn't want that."

"The police will want to preserve the crime scene. We have to stop people entering," I insisted. "Shall I do it? Are you up to it, or do you want to sit down inside? A cup of tea, maybe?"

"Tea? Tea! I don't want tea. I want Del to be alive and for this to all be a dream. You, it's you! I know it must be. I bet you killed those people then pinned the crimes on innocents. Nobody can get caught up in that many murders."

"I'm afraid I can, and I do. I know this sounds mad, but it's Vee, my campervan. It's like ever since I got her, she wants me to travel around and help solve terrible crimes. Help local communities, give people closure. Sorry, it's hard to explain, but I truly am here to help."

"I'm calling the police." Melody swatted my hand away when I held it out to help her up, then clambered to her feet, backed up, and dialled the police, not even realising she was using my phone.

While she answered questions, I made a fuss of Anxious who was fretting because of the lack of attention from Melody and what for him would be an almost overpowering smell of blood. I dared not stray, though, as I didn't want to scare Melody, but also knew that we had to lock the front door and stop people wandering around inside the shop.

With a curt, "Okay," Melody hung up the phone, then handed it to me. "Sorry, I forgot it was yours. Mine's in my apron pocket."

"No problem. Are they on their way?"

"Yes, and they said I was not to disturb the crime scene. Bit late for that now."

Our eyes drifted to the knife, and as Melody bent to retrieve it, I suggested, "Maybe leave it there? The police won't be long."

"Yeah, right. Of course. I'm all flustered. I've never seen a dead body before. Well, once at a funeral, but Grandad was ninety-seven and it was just a glimpse. We better go inside. Can you help me out with something?"

"Of course. Whatever you want." I called for Anxious and we hurried after Melody as she stepped back inside.

She marched down the hall, then stopped beside the office door. "Can you get the keys? They're on the hook over by the desk. Del always kept them there. He was very fastidious about putting everything in its proper place."

"No problem." I glanced at the neat desk as I entered, Anxious right beside me, already in investigating mode, sniffing the floor and doing a circuit of the room. I turned as the door slammed shut behind me, then heard the lock click into place. "Melody, you don't need to do this."

"I do! I don't know you. You might be the killer. I'm going to lock the front door and wait outside. You stay right there until help arrives. If you're a good guy, I'm sorry, but I don't trust you. You obviously know Del, and that wiki page is weird. I bet you wrote it yourself to lure unsuspecting shop assistants to their death. You're a killer!" I heard a barely audible sob then her footsteps retreating.

"Looks like it's just us guys in a stranger's office for a while, Anxious," I sighed, shivering in the cool back room.

Anxious sat and cocked his head, trying to figure out what this latest game was, so I gave him a biscuit and he settled down while I took the opportunity to snoop.

The desk contained a smart Mac, a vape with a charging cable attached to the back of the computer, a notebook, several pens in a chrome container, and a black metal tray for filing paperwork. I sat in the comfortable but battered leather chair and pictured Del writing his note to me then grabbing an envelope, possibly from the drawer, and sealing it. Is that what happened? Melody insisted it was his handwriting, but it was possible it was forged. If so, why? That made even less sense. And it still meant that my location would be known this morning.

Had somebody followed me, then hurried ahead, killed Del, then written the note? How could they have known what I would be doing? There were other shops, and a bakery I might have gone to before the deli. Melody was only a few minutes behind me, so she could have easily found Del first.

I turned to face the wall and noted the window was ajar, but decided it was better not to try to make an escape as that would look very suspicious. A bookshelf contained ledgers and files, presumably containing invoices and orders and the usual admin side of running a business.

On a whim, and without thinking of the consequences, I pressed enter on the keyboard and the screen sprang to life revealing a family photo of Del with a young woman who was clearly his daughter on one side and two teenagers on the other. They were smiling, had deep tans, and judging by the backdrop of sand and high-rise hotels, I assumed they were in the Med somewhere, possibly Spain. Along the bottom of the screen were the usual icons, just for the internet, documents, and the like. I clicked on the Finder icon and then the documents folder, but all that contained was work-related folders and files in order of date and name. Melody was right. Del was an organised man.

Knowing I shouldn't pry, and this was not my place, I clicked X then let the mouse be. Taking my time, I studied the rest of the room, but it was just an office with tired furniture although very neat and tidy. Several more photos of the woman and the children at various ages adorned the walls along with certificates for awards the shop had received over the years. He was clearly as proud of the deli as he was of his family. There were no photos of his wife, though, and I could only assume they were divorced as if she had died surely he would want to keep her memory alive?

A small kitchenette took up the counter to the left of the door, with a fridge beneath, and I realised how thirsty I was. Wondering if this was right or wrong, I nevertheless made myself a coffee then stood drinking, lost to my thoughts, trying to get an angle on this peculiar incident. The sense of it completely eluded me.

I knew for a fact that I hadn't told anyone at the campsite where I was headed; I'd spoken to no one this morning. We'd come into Welshpool on a total whim as when Anxious and I stepped outside for our morning emergency pee, the weather was warm and inviting and it was time for a Crocs celebration. We'd hurried through a cuppa and a quick breakfast, then jumped into Vee and headed into town. I'd not noticed anyone following us, but how else could Del have known we would arrive? Had the killer known too?

No, they couldn't have, as otherwise they would have ensured Del didn't write the note. Was that right? Del knew my route, and how he would die, but nobody else had? If he knew, why write the note rather than do something about it like ensuring he was somewhere else? He even knew which knife would be used. He was right about it too. It was an expensive one. I used the same ones in Vee, and my collection was one of my most prized possessions. They were wrapped up in the roll bag they came with and had been with me for over a decade.

Suddenly I went cold. When did I last use my Shapiro knives? Last night? No, the night before. Yesterday's dinner had been a simple affair of a beef one-pot stew with the meat diced at the butcher's, and I'd prepped the rest with one of the smaller knives from the drawer so hadn't taken notice of if anything was missing. What if it wasn't Del's knife, but mine? That didn't change the fact that he knew in advance what the murder weapon would be.

This was becoming way too confusing. My head swam, I felt dizzy, and I sank into the chair in a cold sweat, stressing that the murder weapon was mine, and with the note I was definitely a suspect even though it asked for my help. The envelope was still out on the counter in the shop, so the police would have it as evidence soon enough, and then I was certain to be in for plenty of dubious questions as the authorities tried to make sense of this crime.

Maybe this time they'd fare better than me, as so far all I could come up with was that Del had written the note after somehow learning about me and my future plans, then had stepped outside and plunged the knife into his own throat before he laid down and bled to death.

Surely a soggy bottomed quiche wouldn't drive a man, even one as proud as Del, to commit suicide? Quiche harakiri? It was far-fetched even for me, and there had been several cases where the motive was beyond strange, but never as peculiar as that.

Next, I considered even more outlandish ideas. Maybe he had a twin? Was it even Del? Was Melody on the level, or was it her all along and she knew me, possibly had seen me in the shop after killing Del, so had nipped inside, written the note to confuse everyone, then raced around to the front door and so the act began? More possible, but why bother? No, the more I thought about this, the more I came to realise that for whatever reason, Del had known about me and his impending death, so had planned this strange encounter.

I wondered why he'd been killed, and why he would accept such a fate so willingly. Something terrible in his past that made him feel he deserved it? Debts? Woman trouble? Family grief? So many questions. Absolutely no answers.

I drained my coffee as I heard a commotion on the other side of the door, and stood as it slammed open and a tall man ducked under the frame and entered, followed by a stout woman with the biggest scowl I'd ever seen.

"You've got a lot of explaining to do, mate," he hissed, noting the empty mug in my hand and raising an eyebrow. "Oh, sorry to disturb your coffee while just outside there's been a murder and so far you're the only suspect."

The woman tutted, then turned to an officer behind them and ordered, "Cuff him. Max Effort, you are under arrest on suspicion of murder."

"You can't be serious?" I gasped, not expecting things to go this far. "I only came in for cheese."

Anxious yipped a correction, tail wagging as he eyed the detectives merrily.

"And a pork pie and possibly some sausage rolls." I held out my hands as the officer pulled out his handcuffs.

Chapter 3

"Gotcha!" laughed the woman.

"Classic," chortled the man.

"Nice one, ma'am," giggled the policeman, giving her the thumbs up before securing his handcuffs at his utility belt.

"It was a joke?" I was beyond confused, and more anxious than my best buddy who sidled forward, sniffed a few pairs of legs, then sat and awaited the inevitable adoration.

"Aw, would you look at the little guy?" The woman, and I assumed a detective like her partner, ignored me completely and bent to stroke Anxious who leaned into it and groaned merrily, his earlier woes forgotten.

"Real cutie," agreed her partner, winking at me like we were sharing an insider joke.

"Traitor," I hissed, then began to relax as at least I wasn't in cuffs.

The woman stood and turned to the officer. "Jones, can you secure the scene out back? We'll be there in a mo. Just need to have a word with the infamous Max Effort here and his wonder dog sidekick."

"Yes, ma'am." The officer turned on his heels and left.

I faced the two detectives, each of us sizing the other up. The woman I judged to be in her early forties. She was a no-nonsense dresser with a somewhat faded black suit, a white blouse, and running trainers which I wondered why more didn't wear as if you're on your feet all day they would ease some of the inevitable aches and pains. She had a simple haircut of a bob to her shoulders with a straight fringe above her darkly made-up blue eyes. Her clear complexion and faint laughter lines revealed she often smiled, and she was clearly amused by her prank.

Her partner was closing on sixty, with jeans that looked like a supermarket buy, no pretence at acting like he cared about fashion, confirmed by his budget blue shirt. His eyes sparkled, were very intense and so pale I was reminded of ice, but he had a lot of wrinkles and a very dark tan, so I knew he was a sun worshipper and had most likely just returned from holidaying somewhere nice. He noted me studying him and his eyes travelled down to the dull black shoes scuffed at the toes. One lace was undone.

"Never did care much about fashion," he acknowledged. "The wife and kids always make fun of me for looking like I do my clothes shopping in Sainsbury's, and I remind them that she was the one who bought everything."

"Under your instruction, you saddo," teased his partner. "You need to do your own clothes shopping, or at least stop insisting she buy you the same damn stuff year after year. Ever heard of Vinted? Or at least eBay?"

"I like what I like, and what I like is the familiar. I'm not good with change, you know that. And besides, everything always gets wrecked, so why spend the money on clothes when I can spend it on holidays?"

"Fair enough. Wish I could have a few weeks in the sun."

"That's your decision," he grunted, but the affection between the two was clear. "If you spent less on your dumb van and saved more, you could go abroad too."

"Don't you call my van dumb. Transit Customs are the perfect vehicle. I can fit in the parking spaces at Asda, but still go anywhere I want and sleep in it. I love it and wouldn't swap it for the world. Friday night, I finished work, drove without even knowing where I was going, and found an awesome spot in the middle of nowhere. I walked in the woods in the dark, cooked on my little stove, and had an awesome night's sleep. You can't get that on the Costas."

"No, but you can get someone else to do the cooking and have a proper bed in a hotel and some actual sun. This winter has been bleak and beyond wet. It isn't right."

"Tell me about it," she agreed, smiling at him.

Beyond confused by their conversation and that they'd seemingly forgotten about me, it suddenly clicked that maybe this was an act, like good cop, good cop or something, and they were teasing me. Regardless, I had to ask, "Did you convert the Transit yourself? Long wheel base or short?"

"Short. Like I said, makes it easy to use as my regular vehicle. I just put in a diesel heater and it makes all the difference. But I refuse to have electricity. What's the point? I don't go away to want everything the same as at home. And I have my power bank anyway for charging phones and whatnot."

"Blimey, you two, get a room!" The detective laughed at his own joke, then slowly his smile faded and he nodded to his partner who returned the gesture.

"Sorry about that, Max. And yes, we know your name, read the note, and did a little checking into you. Actually, I'd heard of you anyway. You have quite the reputation. You ruffled some feathers in these parts, and right up on the north coast too. We know all about you."

"I'd never heard of the guy. I read your wiki page though. Very interesting. So, solved it yet?" he taunted, looking smug.

"Not yet," I huffed, unsure about what would happen next. "Um, I'm really not under arrest? You were messing?"

"Course not," laughed the woman. "Max, we might not have a clue what is going on here, but we don't believe you killed the guy after somehow getting him to write a note addressed to you asking for your help. And what's with the soggy bottom?"

"I know, right? I mean, he clearly knew that you pre-bake the pastry."

"Really? Never knew that. I meant, why mention it? Bit weird, isn't it? Oh, hey, sorry, we never introduced ourselves. I'm Laura, this is Bishop."

"Like in Aliens? I hope you aren't a robot."

"Bishop was played by Sigourney Weaver," Bishop snapped. "It's a common misconception. For some reason, people misremember."

"That's not right. Sigourney Weaver was Ripley. Bishop was the robot."

Laura wagged a finger and said, "Bishop wasn't a robot. He was an android, and he preferred to be called an artificial person. You're both wrong."

"I stand corrected," said Bishop, smiling. I was convinced he knew exactly who his namesake was.

"Why did you do that?" I couldn't help asking. "Pretend you didn't know who Bishop was in the Aliens movie?"

"He got you there," laughed Laura. "Max, we do that little act, if anyone bothers to mention Bishop's name, to see if you have any backbone and are certain of your own mind. Under stress, most people forget their own names, let alone their age or where they live. You've got a level head even though you are in a whole heap of trouble. Well done."

"Um, thanks, I guess. So, can I go?"

Laura and Bishop exchanged a glance, then burst out laughing.

"Something funny?" I asked, a sinking feeling in my stomach.

"Max, you might not be under arrest, but you most definitely are coming down to the station to answer a ridiculously long list of questions. You've been linked to no end of murders, and yes, we know you helped solve them, but this is different. Someone was murdered and they seemingly knew you. They wrote you a letter asking for your help, knew your whereabouts, even how they would be killed. We've already searched the kitchen here and the Shapiro knives are all there as far as we can tell. Melody thinks so too."

"I did wonder if my knife was used," I admitted, thinking it would be churlish to pretend otherwise.

"We aren't saying it was your knife, but are you saying you own the exact same one?"

"I didn't get a close enough look at it to be a hundred percent sure, but most likely, yes. It's a quality Japanese knife, and I have a set in a roll bag. It's leather. It's very common for chefs."

"So you're under suspicion, even though we aren't saying we think you did this. We have to go by the book. Understand?"

"I do, yes. Is Melody okay? She freaked out and locked me in here, but I hope she's coping."

"She's shaken up, confused, and scared. She did the right thing, even if you might feel differently."

"I don't. I understand she was worried I might attack her. Should we go now?"

Bishop stepped into the room properly and said, "Why don't you make yourself another coffee? Stay put, and once we've finished here we'll come with you back to the station. Otherwise, we can get one of the officers to take you now, but you'll be stuck in an interview room for hours. Your choice."

"I'll wait here. I suppose I better tell you. I had a quick look at his computer. I didn't find anything."

They both frowned, but let it pass, then Laura said, "You'll have to stay by the kettle while we search the room, and we'll bag up his Mac to take to the station. It always takes forever to go through the computers. A right chore."

"The worst," agreed Bishop. "I preferred it when it was just a paper trail."

"That's because you're old and decrepit."

"I am not! I'm in my prime. Not even sixty."

"You're fifty-nine! Old."

"Are you two always like this?" I asked.

"How'd you mean?" asked Laura.

"Like what?" asked Bishop.

"Um, such fun? You seem really close. Laura, can I ask? How's the diesel heater? I just went through a freezing winter and never found the time to get one fitted. I was thinking about it, as we've still got a few cold months ahead."

"Best investment ever. Don't get a cheap one, and don't get one too powerful either, but well worth it. Fitted mine myself. Saved a few hundred quid that way."

"There will be plenty of time for van talk later. Right now, we have an investigation to start." Bishop nodded to Laura and cast a warning glance my way, then they were all business and called for the computer to be taken. While I made coffee for myself, they inspected the room, took endless photos, and then I was stuck in the corner, watching as a forensics team went over the whole room thoroughly. It was fascinating, but after a while I went to leave but was warned the DIs had insisted I stay put so that's what Anxious and I did.

For hours.

Anxious grew so bored that he resorted to lying upside down on the now cleared desk, legs akimbo, head hanging over the side, his tongue lolling as he whimpered in his sleep. I was tempted to join him but instead drank coffee and thought about the case.

Del was moved eventually, carried away in a bag on a stretcher, the teams seemingly finished with him, although I knew more extensive investigations would take place at the mortuary. It wasn't a nice thing; there was no peace in death for victims of violent crime.

Slowly the teams packed up and left, and as the young officer guarding the door drifted away and I was left alone, I poked my head out into the corridor and found nobody there so decided to stretch my legs as who knew when I'd be allowed to actually leave. My stomach rumbled as I crept into the shop, the smell of Del's amazing goodies enticing and teasing me; it would go to waste unless something was done.

With the shop empty, and no sign of a police presence, I wandered back through the building then outside and found the DIs standing beside where Del had been found, talking quietly. I cleared my throat and they glanced up then ignored me and continued their conversation before nodding to each other and approaching.

"Sorry about the wait, Max, but as you already know, this one is a real head-scratcher."

"It's fine. I understand. Have you found anything out? Did anyone see Del come to work this morning, or see him leave? Somehow, he knew my location, so I wondered if he'd followed me. I don't know why he would, but clearly something isn't right about any of this. Actually, it's creeping me out."

"That's a good call," said Laura, glancing at Bishop with an approving nod.

"You clearly understand how these things work," said Bishop. "Max, we've had coppers doing the rounds and asking about, and Del was seen like he was every morning. He had a strict routine, and hardly ever strayed from it. The guy from the corner shop is always there early to sort out the newspapers, although I didn't even know people still had them delivered, so he shared a few words with Del. It's a regular thing. He never saw him again, and neither did anyone else as far as we can ascertain. Inquiries will continue, and there are a few CCTV cameras dotted about the high street, so those will be checked."

"So how did he know I'd come to the shop?"

"That's what we'd like to know, Max. Time to get you to the station and take a proper statement. You good with that?" By Bishop's tone, it was clear I was going whether I wanted to or not.

"Sure. Should I drive, or do I have to come with you guys?"

"You can drive. We're doing this on trust, understand?" Laura brushed her hair back over tiny ears and fixed a no-nonsense gaze on me.

"You can trust me."

"We hope so."

We made the arrangements, then I went to get Anxious and joined them in the shop where they unlocked the door and I left, pleased to find the sun still shining and the street busy with people going about their everyday business. It was coming up on lunchtime now, and I was famished, so once we got back to Vee, my beautiful campervan, I rifled through what was left in the tiny, some would say often annoying fridge, and fixed myself a rather uninspiring sandwich. I longed for the offerings in the deli, but there was no chance of making a purchase now.

After I'd eaten, and tidied up, I sat with Anxious on the bench seat, the familiarity and sense of safety settling my nerves. Vee was my home, my sanctuary, a place I knew intimately as even by campervan standards it was small. Classic VWs looked awesome, were very well laid out, and perfect for travelling around in, but there was no escaping the cramped conditions if you spent much time inside.

Not that I did. Whenever possible, I was outside enjoying the British countryside or the sights that still left me breathless, and with my new and improved gazebo life had been even more comfortable than ever, but right now I was happy to sit inside and feel cocooned in the metal box with my best buddy beside me.

The last thing I wanted to do was to keep the DIs waiting, as so far they'd been kind and easygoing compared to many I'd encountered, so with a sigh, I fixed Anxious into the seatbelt clip then clambered into the front and got going.

Once I was processed at the station, I was led into a spotless back room that contained a table perpendicular to the side wall, four metal chairs, and nothing else. I only had to wait for ten minutes then the DIs arrived and asked if I needed anything, but I was good so they sat and did the preliminary talking into the microphone giving the time and date and who was present, then the interview began.

Although not exactly a stranger to these proceedings, I still got the same sense of being slightly unnerved. No matter that I knew I was innocent, being interviewed by the authorities still left me rather stressed and worried I'd get accused of something and have to be locked up. The DIs were kind, but blunt with their questions, and I had to give a full account of my whereabouts that morning and for the previous few days as best I could remember, then we got down to the real nitty gritty.

"How did Del know about you, Max?"

"I have no idea. I'd never heard of the deli until I chanced on it this morning. It was my first time in town and I had no plans when I set out."

"You didn't talk to anyone and tell them you were going there?"

"No, absolutely not. I didn't know, so how could I? I just wanted to get some nice food and have a wander around. I saw the deli, we went inside, and then Melody arrived. She said the door should have been locked."

"That's what she told us. Look, Max, we're going to be honest with you here." Laura glanced at Bishop and he nodded.

"I'm not going to like this, am I?"

"Probably not. Here's the deal. This makes absolutely no sense unless someone wrote that note once Del was killed. The only logical explanation here is that as you were the first one inside the shop, you found Del, then for whatever twisted reason you went into his office, copied his handwriting, and wrote that note. It's the only possible explanation."

"Wait. What!? You're saying I wrote it?"

"It's the logical conclusion," said Bishop. "You found Del, you scribbled the letter, then Melody appeared and you acted like you didn't know anything about it."

"Why would I do that? And don't forget, the door out to the back was locked from the inside. I didn't have a key."

"There were keys in the office, so that's easy enough to explain."

"Okay, maybe that's true, but why would I write the note? Are you saying I killed him?"

"We aren't saying you killed him, but I am guessing that your fingerprints will be the only ones on the envelope and the paper."

"Because Melody handed it to me. Her fingerprints will be on it too."

"Sure, but she isn't in for questioning right now, is she?" asked Laura. "Why did you do it, Max? Been missing the intrigue, have you? According to your wiki page, you haven't been involved in a murder for over two months. Getting withdrawal symptoms from the murder mysteries is our best guess. You wanted to be involved, so when you found the corpse, you wrote the note. That way, you're part of this."

"I didn't do it." I crossed my arms and glared at them, but they were unperturbed and merely shrugged, keeping silent, playing the trick where they say nothing in the hopes their suspect would continue talking. I never said another word.

Time passed, until eventually Bishop asked, "Do you want to confess and get this over with? We don't believe you killed Del, but the message is so dumb. It must have been you who wrote it. You wanted in on the investigation and this way you get what you wanted. Del asked for you by name, addressed it to you, so either you did whatever it took so you could help look into this, or…"

"Or?" I asked, feeling there was a ray of hope waiting.

Laura nodded to Bishop, so he said, "Or Del really did want your help. How and why is a real mystery."

"So let me help figure this out."

Another exchanged look, then both sighed and Laura said, "Fine, but there are caveats."

"A lot of them," agreed Bishop.

I could finally breathe properly. I was in the clear.
For now.

Chapter 4

"Feeling relieved?" laughed Bishop, looking like a load had been taken off and wiping his forehead with a white handkerchief.

"Very," I admitted. "I really thought you were going to lock me up. I know this is beyond weird, but you do believe me, don't you?"

"We do, and we did all along, Max." Laura gave the time the interview finished then turned off the recording. "Right, now that's done, let's get down to it."

"How'd you mean? And you did believe me? Why all this then?"

"Because we're detectives, and this is how things work. We needed an official statement, and to ensure you were on the level. Max, we've spoken to a few people about you, and although several were annoyed, they all said the same thing. You're a nice, genuine guy. We had to check you weren't up to no good, but we're satisfied this is exactly how it seems."

"Which is?"

Bishop placed his hands on the table, leaned forward, his partner joining him, and told me, "That someone murdered Del and somehow he knew it was going to happen and how it would be done, and that you would find him. We don't have the foggiest how that could be true, but it is. That's it. Sorry about getting heavy with you, but I'm sure you understand."

"This wasn't your normal start to an investigation," said Laura. "It's got everyone scratching their heads, and our boss is already breathing down our necks over this. You have to keep this quiet, as the last thing we want is word getting out about Del's note."

"I won't tell a soul. What happens now? Can I look into this? Should I?"

"If we tell you not to, will you do as you're told?" asked Bishop, eyes twinkling with mirth as he clearly already knew the answer.

"Doubtful," I laughed. "My name is quite literally all over this, and I want to know why. The poor man is dead, and I'm still concerned about the knife. Did you look into that?"

"Of course we did! Rest easy, Max. We checked out your gazebo, and it's a nice set-up by the way, very professional." Laura smiled, clearly appreciative of anything to do with vanlife.

"Thanks. I like a tidy kitchen."

"I'm jealous. Anyway, all your knives were there, assuming it was just the one set of Shapiro?"

"It was. So it was probably one of Del's?"

"Most likely. He was rather more random with his kitchen, although tidy enough, but he had a few sets, some mismatched, and the note said it was his, so· we can confirm that."

"What do you both think? Why get me involved? How?"

"Guess he liked how you solved mysteries," said Bishop. "The tech guys are still going over his Mac, but his recent browsing history has your wiki page, so he definitely knew of you. Nothing else apart from the usual, but they'll keep looking."

"Thanks for being so open with me. And I understand why you tried to get me to confess. It would have made this case much easier, right?"

"Much!" Laura smirked at Bishop.

"What's going on?" I asked.

"Nothing. We're intrigued, is all. We're interested to see how you go about trying to solve this. It's unlike anything we've ever encountered, and we've been on the job a long time. Bishop here has been a detective for decades. He could be sitting in an office running things, but he likes to do proper investigating, and I've been a DI for over a decade. We do good work, but this is something way beyond what we usually encounter."

"So we want to see how you do," said Bishop. "You're free to go, but we'd appreciate you staying in touch, and we'll be checking in on you regularly. Time to get to work, Max."

"I have your blessing?"

"No, you absolutely do not!" chuckled Laura. "Keep a low profile, stay out of our way, and be sure to tell us if you find anything. We got a deal?"

"You have a deal."

Both rose, and we shook hands, then I was told I could go so got out of there as fast as possible.

I was so shell-shocked and unnerved by being in the station and the way the interview went, that once I'd taken Anxious for a quick walk as he was desperate for a pee, I simply sat in Vee in the police station car park for a few minutes then made myself a strong cup of coffee and perched on the step and drank it slowly, trying to put recent events into some kind of order that made sense.

I failed miserably.

Usually, I was an upbeat kind of guy, but knowing I had to return to the campsite, pack up the kitchen, dismantle the gazebo, then figure out what to do next left me rather down in the dumps. My carefree attitude meant I had numerous adventures travelling around finding the next great spot to stay, but I was rather out of the loop after spending several months in the same place, and should have thought ahead.

Quite often I left it until the day before I had to leave somewhere to find the next spot, but I'd decided to wait until today and now I'd have to find a site at short notice. I'd been surprised when the place I was at only allowed me a few days as they were fully booked for today and the next few days, but apparently it was the same every year, with people deciding March was the time to get out into the country and shake out the sleeping bags, dust off the tents, or give their vans or caravans a good airing and wake them from their winter slumber.

With no other choice, I sighed, then sorted out the coffee stuff as the last thing you want when driving are things flying everywhere. Even the smallest item becomes a missile when you brake hard or have an accident.

"Hello," called Melody.

I turned and smiled to show there were no bad feelings, and she relaxed instantly and returned the smile.

"Hi."

"You aren't cross with me, are you?"

"Of course not. You were scared, and unsure about me, so I understand why you locked me in the office. You did the right thing. What are you doing here?"

"They had me in for questioning. I was in there for hours. The detectives spoke to me earlier, then left, I presume to speak to you, then they returned and we went over everything again. I think we're the two main suspects."

"They're just doing their job. We were the ones who found Del, and what with the note and everything it makes sense they'd suspect us."

"Did they give you a lot of grief?"

"Not really. Just wanted to make sure I hadn't killed him, then written the note."

"Why would you do that?"

"Why would whoever did this kill him? Why would Del write the message and let himself get murdered?"

"It's so dumb, isn't it? I mean, what got into him? The police took my fingerprints and asked about the knife. I told them I panicked and pulled it out, but that looked bad for me."

"They asked me about it too. The best thing is always to tell the truth. Then you know you aren't hiding anything."

"I did tell them the truth. Anyway, I just wanted to say sorry. Are you okay? You look a little fed up. How's Anxious?"

His ears perked up at the mention of his name, so he hopped down, stretched out, then padded over to Melody and sat in front of her.

"Coping very well. Unfortunately, he's quite used to death. We seem to encounter a lot of it. But he's helped so much uncovering the killers, and I'm sure he'll help again this time."

Melody paused from stroking his head and lifted her eyes until they met mine. "So you're going to investigate? Like, for real? Try to solve the murder?"

"Absolutely. The DIs said as long as I didn't interfere with their investigation, I can look into it. Why does that surprise you so much?"

"Max, are you serious? People don't do that. Regular folk do not investigate murders."

"I'm not regular people. I know I told you before, but I do think it's my calling. I roam, I help when I can."

"Because the van makes you?" she teased, eyeing up the interior. "It is very nice. I love the retro feel. Did you do it?"

"Most of it is original. I fixed some of the upholstery, but not too much else. It's freezing in the winter as it doesn't have proper insulation, is slow, and noisy on the roads. Sometimes she's unpredictable, but I adore Vee and wouldn't change her for anything."

"That's so sweet. So, what next?"

I explained about the campsite, and that I had to leave, and as I spoke, she began to smile. "What's so amusing?" I asked.

"Let me come and give you a hand packing up, then I have the perfect solution for you. I assume you want something for at least a few days, if not longer, depending on how fast you 'solve' the case?"

"Did you just do air quotes?" I laughed, finally warming to Melody after the less than ideal start to our pending friendship.

"I might have. Max, are you serious? You really will try to figure out who killed Del and what this is all about?"

"I'm serious. Can I be honest with you?"

"I hope so. I'm deep into this, too, you know. Say whatever you want."

"I know this sounds terrible, and of course I'm so sorry about Del, and I know you thought an awful lot of him, but I miss solving mysteries. I spent two months helping a couple renovate a Georgian farmhouse at their new campsite, and loved the work, and being in one place, but it was quite lonely at times. I missed using my brain and helping people in other ways."

"Solving murders?"

"Exactly. It's what I'm meant to do. I have a good eye for detail and try my best to help people, and that's what I'm going to do now. As long as you don't mind, of course."

"If you can figure this out, I'm all for it. Del was a dear friend and a truly wonderful man. He looked after me for so long, gave me a steady job with a decent wage, and was always kind. We got on really well and had such a laugh. There was always a lot of stress, of course, as that's part of running a business, but we were happy."

"Can we talk later about his personal life, and maybe yours? Right now, I have to go and pack up, and if you don't mind helping that would be great."

"I can't go back to work, so keeping busy is important. Let's go."

Melody had been given a lift in a police car, leaving hers back in town, so we went in Vee, bumping along the track up to the campsite where my gazebo and outdoor kitchen were now squashed between a huge motorhome with a family of five outside having a late lunch, and a VW Transporter on the other.

As was always the case, I spent a few minutes talking to a fellow VDubber as there was never any avoiding that, then Melody helped me to load everything into Vee and dismantle the gazebo. It didn't take long, but by the time we'd finished there was already another van waiting to take the spot we would soon vacate.

I waved at the couple, then we got into Vee, buckled up, and I drove up towards the main gate so they could set up. I parked up so we could have a chat, and asked, "Why is it so busy? It's March, not summer. Other places aren't like this yet. It will be months before you're fighting for a spot, and even then there are plenty of campsites where they're half empty."

"It's a tradition around here. Most are locals coming to unwind and take it easy for a while because of the holiday. It only lasts a week, then the place is back to being dead. This is one of the main sites, so is always the worst."

"How do you know so much about it?"

"Because I have a sister who is an absolute camping nut. She's not so into the vanlife, she has a nice house and a husband and kids, but she has a little Berlingo and is off whenever she can. She loves camping."

"You not so much?"

"I like it well enough, but I'm always busy with work or trying to recover from the long days. I don't know how she does it with the family to look after."

"What about you? Husband? Children?"

"There was a husband, but we're divorced. No children. Looks like I missed that boat unless I find the perfect man in the next few seconds and we decide to have children. I'm pushing forty, so my time's almost up."

"Sorry to hear that."

"Don't be. I've never been happier. That's all ruined now, of course, but I'll manage. I've always been good with money, so have plenty saved, and even have rental income from a flat I bought before prices went nuts. I'll be fine."

"I have rental income too. It's how I can live like this."

"Max, no offence, but I don't think we're in the same league. You were a fancy pants chef with a big house and all the trappings of wealth. I have a tiny flat I get a few quid for every month."

"Sorry if I caused offence. I didn't mean to."

"That's fine. I was just setting things straight."

I smiled at Melody, appreciating her no-nonsense approach. She told it like she saw it, and I admired the bluntness. "Okay, so what's the deal with you and Del? Were you ever more than just boss and staff member? What was your job title?"

"Job title? Are you kidding?" Melody shook her head, her hair flying everywhere, the smell of apple shampoo and her perfume strong. I immediately thought of Min and had to hide my smile, as I recalled how she hated it when I sniffed her hair and said it was weird. Of course it wasn't!

"You had no title?"

"I worked in the deli. That was my title. Woman that works in the deli. Shop assistant, I suppose. And as for our relationship, he was over twenty years older, rather overweight, and had hair growing on his back. I know some women love the bear look, but I like my men tall, brooding, and handsome."

"Right. Sorry to ask."

"And before you get all weirded out, just so you know, you aren't my type."

"I'm not?" I raised an eyebrow. Maybe I wasn't the most handsome guy, but I thought I looked okay.

"No. For a start, I read about you and Min, and would never go after another woman's bloke. But you're too tall, you have too much hair on that pretty head of yours, and you live in a tiny van. No thank you." Melody giggled and nudged me in the ribs, then shook her head. "You don't know how handsome you are, do you? That's so sweet.

Max, you're gorgeous, but truly not my type. I like my guys wiry and with short hair and stubble."

"That's a very specific type. Anything else? And thank you for the compliment. I'm not the best at receiving them, but I appreciate it. And you're a very pretty woman. Any man would be lucky to have you as a girlfriend."

"Aw, that's sweet. Now, let's get out of here, shall we?" Melody fluttered her eyelashes, teasing me, and laughed.

"It's nice to hear you laugh. I know today was awful. I promise I'll do my best to uncover the truth."

"Hey, not so fast, mister. If you're involved, then how do you think I feel? We're a team on this, and I won't take no for an answer. If you want to investigate, I'm pleased, but no way am I letting you do it alone. You good with that?"

"Not really, as I wouldn't want anything to happen to you. There's a murderer on the loose."

"I can look after myself."

"I'm sure you can." I noted the set of her jaw and how her fists were bunched. Melody had already made up her mind. "Then yes, two heads will be better than one. But promise me you won't do anything to put yourself in danger?"

"Scout's honour. So, I'll give you directions, and you just drive."

"Where are we going? What's this about? Shouldn't you tell me where I'm going to be living for the next few days?"

"It's a surprise. Trust me, you'll love it. You do trust me, don't you, Max?"

"I do. As much as I trust anyone I met a few hours ago who locked me in a room."

"Then it's settled. We both trust each other, but only enough to work together and see how this thing goes."

"You tell it straight, don't you?"

"You better believe it! I don't mince words, and I don't lie. So if you're easily offended, you better watch out."

"We're going to get on just fine, Melody. As long as you don't make me set up in a field full of pigs or anything."

"Just drive," she ordered, winking.

So I did just that.

Chapter 5

Vee purred along nicely, as though she was happy with wherever we were headed. At first I was apprehensive, but with Melody sitting beside me and grinning the whole time, Anxious curled up and snoring on the back seat, and Vee coping with the hills and winding roads without issue, I let my concerns fade and just enjoyed the ride and company.

Melody gave instructions as we headed away from town and into the countryside proper, although the beauty of our location was that pretty much everything was countryside. Only a stone's throw from the West Midlands, we were in Wales but only just, and I thought I knew the whole area very well. Turned out I was wrong, and although we didn't travel far, we were certainly straying from my usual haunts.

"Turn here," said Melody, the words now very familiar.

"You sure?" I asked, noting the chain-link fence stretching along either side of the track that seemed to enter a woodland.

"Yep," she said smugly.

With a shrug, I indicated and did as I was told, expecting her to tell me to park up for a spot of stealth camping. We bumped along the track, then passed through a large opening where the gates had been removed and emerged instantly into a vast expanse of open ground.

"It's an old airfield. Not many people are even aware it's here, and it's become quite popular with those in the know." Melody grinned as she tapped her nose. "Keep it quiet, don't tell anyone, and enjoy."

"Is it abandoned?"

"For years. There's the main airfield right by town, but this old place was shut long before that even opened. Used to be tarmac, but the grass and weeds reclaimed it and then the trees sprouted. Amazing what nature can do, eh? There's no stopping it reclaiming what it once had."

"Incredible. What a place. It's huge."

"I know, and perfect for vanlifers or anyone wanting to stay somewhere nice on the cheap. And by cheap, I mean free. It might not have services like fancy campsites, but you can't beat the price."

I drove across the incredibly flat surface, amazed at how green it was and the number of trees that'd battled to survive then thrive in such conditions, but you truly would never have known it used to be for planes. Various grasses, wild plants, saplings, and mature trees had somehow flourished, and people had taken advantage and picked idyllic spots to set up with their vans and motorhomes of all description.

"How many people stay here?"

"Gosh, who knows? My sister, the camping nut, told me about it years ago. She comes sometimes, although it's not easy to pitch a tent here because of the ground, but she reckons there are about twenty or so vans here all year. Some live here full-time, others use it as a base, and loads stay for a few nights."

"And there's no trouble? Is it legal?"

"Let's just say nobody will bother you here. It isn't legal and it isn't illegal, if you get my drift. It's not exactly stealth camping, but the authorities don't mind. It's one of those unwritten things, where everyone would prefer people to stay here than in a lay-by or in the towns, so it's passed over and everyone can get on with their lives. You like?"

"It's perfect. I'll find a spot." It didn't take long to find the ideal place close to a large beech tree and well away from everyone else. You certainly had the room to spread out here.

Melody seemed keen to help, so we got busy setting up the gazebo and outdoor kitchen, although it was a struggle to get the pegs for the guy ropes into the ground but I managed as the old tarmac had been broken into tiny chunks by the grass and weeds.

Twenty minutes later, we were done, and stood back to admire the set-up I was as familiar with now as the back of my hands.

"Perfect." Melody held up a hand and we high-fived.

"Thank you so much for all your help. This will be ideal for a few days while we look into things."

Melody took the offered coffee I'd made, then we settled in the camping chairs outside the gazebo and looked out at the private site home to dozens of people and their various vehicles so spread out it was hard to make out more than dabs of colour.

"Ah, that's good. Maybe this vanlife isn't so bad after all. But what about electric? Gosh, sorry, Max, I didn't even think."

"I've had electric hookup for months to run my heater, but I have a good power bank and solar so I'll use that if I need to. It's warm enough at the moment that I should be okay without heating. I'll use my hot water bottle, and Anxious runs hot so we can cuddle up."

"I bet you do no matter what the weather's like."

I chuckled, then agreed, "Try keeping him off the bed. He has his own pillow and everything."

"What now? Where do we start?"

"You want to look into this straight away?" I raised an eyebrow, still unsure how keen Melody was to go down this rabbit hole. "You know this might be upsetting, and dangerous, right? That it might uncover things you'd rather not learn? Whatever the reason he was killed, it won't be nice. You sure about this?"

"I'm absolutely sure. Max, he was my friend. Actually, my best friend. He deserves justice. I know the detectives will do their best, and let's hope they figure this out. Maybe there's stuff on his computer, but he wasn't big into tech, or maybe they'll find some other clue that will help, but I want to do something too. I need to. I owe it to Del. You understand?"

"Of course I do. Then it's settled. We should begin right back where this started. At the deli. Hey, what about the food? It's such a shame it will go to waste."

Melody frowned, then her face kind of crumpled and a single tear rolled down her cheek before she wiped it away. "Del will be turning in his grave. He lived for that place, and took great pride in what he did. Not just what he made himself, or I helped with, but the offerings from other local businesses. He never saw it as competition, and was always happy to showcase bread from the bakers, meat from the butchers, local jams, honey, chutney, you name it. He imported quite a bit, too, but only from places he had a personal connection to. Whenever he took a holiday, which wasn't very often, it would be to visit small producers in other countries to check they had the best welfare for animals and they were genuine. He was great."

"I wish I could have met him. He sounds like a fine man. We'll figure this out, Melody. What did the police say about the food? And what about the business? Who will get it now?"

"I'm not sure. I never discussed such things with him. He has an ex-wife, but they don't get on. She was a nasty piece of work, apparently. They split just before I started working for him. But his daughter is lovely. Bonnie's about your age. She has two stunning daughters. Early teens, as she had them when she was young. He doted on all three of them and they're always around." Melody's hand slapped to her mouth and she gasped. "I didn't even think to call her. She'll be distraught."

"That's okay. I'm sure she has someone with her. You know her well?"

"Quite well. She has her own thing going on and is always busy. We see more of the girls than his daughter, but she's a nice woman. Maybe she'll inherit. I suppose she will."

"Then we need to visit her. I know this is hard, but someone did this and we can't rule anyone out. It isn't personal."

"Of course it's personal," bristled Melody. "Sorry, I didn't mean to snap, but, Max, don't you get it? This absolutely is personal. Someone murdered my boss, my friend, that poor woman's father, and the twins' grandfather. They ruined a business, killed him in the worst manner possible. It's personal."

"You're right, and I apologise. Now, what did the police say about the shop? About the food and everything?"

"That it would be up to the next of kin. They've done their checks, gone over the scene, but they aren't interested in the food. I think the office and some other stuff is out of bounds, we aren't to touch it, but the perishables aren't seen as assets. The preserved goods have value, but anything that will rot is worthless in a day or two. It would be stealing to take anything that will keep, but not food that will be no good soon."

"I think we should get back to the shop and take it from there. Now we know we're both on the level, we can take a proper look around without wondering if the other one is the killer. Agreed?"

"Agreed." With a smile, Melody squeezed my hand.

Anxious came trotting back over, a massive grin on his face. He sat facing us, cocked his head, then figured he'd try his old trick again. He raised a paw and whined, eyes darting briefly to me with a wink, then focused on Melody and whined again.

"He's so cute. Are you sure he's alright? He looks like he's really hurt."

Stifling a giggle, I said, "Watch this." I pointed off to the side and belted out, "Rabbits!"

Anxious leaped to his feet, his head snapped around, and he tore off in the direction I'd pointed.

"Guess he's not too badly injured," laughed Melody, her sadness forgotten for a moment.

"Not too badly," I agreed, smiling at her. "When he comes back, we'll head back into town. You have keys, right?"

"Yes, to everything. Max, what happens to Del now?"

"His daughter will most likely confirm it's him, although you already did that, and a funeral will be arranged." I didn't go into detail, as who wants to know what goes on in a murder case?

"Everyone will be so upset."

"We'll visit anyone you think is important in his life. We need to talk about enemies, or people he's had a disagreement with, but that can wait. Ah, here's Anxious now."

The little guy came racing back, tongue lolling, then collapsed beside me, chest heaving. "Did you catch it?" I teased, winking at Melody who tried not to laugh. When I got no response, we left him to recover while we stowed the chairs, I rinsed out the cups and zipped up the gazebo, then called for Anxious who decided he wanted to cuddle up with Melody so they both got into the front seat.

Time to get back into the thick of it. I just hoped my taste buds could cope with a return to the deli and the food that would have been sold today.

Our return trip was a much more sombre affair. Melody was lost to her dark thoughts, so I didn't disturb her, and merely soaked up the beautiful surroundings. Wales truly was a beautiful country, and as I often had, I wondered why it had never become the tourist hotspot that Cornwall and Devon had. Maybe the inaccessibility once you got away from the South Wales M4 corridor, or possibly the often torturous drive from the east to the west coast and the beautiful beaches.

From Llandudno in the north to St Davids and as far down as Cardigan Bay, there were no end of stunning beaches and seaside towns to choose from, and although always busy in season, it was still nothing like Cornwall. It suited me just fine, and I was glad to be back. Rolling hills, rugged cliffs, friendly people, excellent cuisine, no end of local culture and quirks, it had everything a vanlifer could want. Apart from traffic lights.

I pulled to a stop at a set of temporary ones, and recalled seeing them five years ago on a trip with Min. The side of the road had collapsed, turning the already narrow point into a single lane, and seemingly the council budget or whoever paid for such things hadn't stretched to getting it repaired yet. But how much did it cost to keep the lights running for so many years? A true mystery, and one I knew even I with my knack for solving the seemingly unsolvable wouldn't have a hope of figuring out. The paper trail was probably longer than the road we were waiting on.

Nevertheless, the lights changed soon enough and minutes later I had parked and we were walking back to Del's Deli, Anxious with a spring in his step, nose in the air, sniffing all the enticing smells he could as we approached.

Melody paused outside the shop, eyes downcast, keys in hand, so I asked, "Are you sure you want to do this? You can always go home and get some rest. We could try again later, or possibly tomorrow. Or never if it's too painful."

Her eyes rose and she shook her head. "No, I want to do this now. The sooner we do it, the more chance of us discovering a clue. And we need to figure out what to do with the food. We can't sell it, as we aren't allowed to be open as it isn't my business, but I was told I could do what I wanted with the food. Take whatever you want, but I can't accept any money."

"That doesn't feel right. It would be like stealing, or taking advantage of Del."

"Trust me, Del would want you to have it. You're an ex-chef, and clearly know what it takes to be as good as him, so he'd want you to fill your boots."

Anxious nudged me with his nose, somehow understanding, and encouraging me to at least nab all the sausage rolls and hand them over.

"Someone wouldn't mind a few treats," I laughed, nodding to the salivating Jack Russell.

"Then, Anxious, it is your lucky day. Although sausages aren't the best for dogs usually. There's garlic and onion in lots, but Del made ones that are suitable for humans and dogs, so let's see what we can find, shall we?"

Anxious barked his agreement, as although he might not have understood everything that was said, he certainly knew the word sausage when he heard it. As if to prove his point, he scrabbled at the door, then turned his head and implored Melody with a look to open up.

"Fine, don't be in such a rush," she laughed, then pulled out her keys from her small bag. As she moved to unlock the door, Anxious' weight pushed it open and he barked for joy then shot inside.

"I thought the police said they'd lock up when they left?" I asked. "The crime scene tape is still up, so this is weird."

"They promised me they had. The whole place might have been ransacked. Hurry!"

Before I could grab her and encourage caution, she shoved on the door and raced inside. I chased after her and managed to put a hand to her shoulder and warned, "Careful. We don't know who's in here. It could be anyone."

"Like the murderer?"

"Who knows?"

We stood stock still, and checked out the shop, but as far as I could tell everything was as it should be. No food had gone, nothing was broken, and there was no sign of forced entry on the door. We sighed with relief and then I hurried to Anxious who was on his hind legs and sniffing the counter; he knew better than that as he could contaminate the food and most likely would have been told to leave this morning if Del had been alive to witness his antics.

"Stay on all fours, please. No stealing food. You can have something later."

Anxious dropped back and hung his head, looking guilty for a millisecond before grinning and locking his focus on the sausage rolls.

Melody was standing stock still in the middle of the room, turning slowly as if taking it all in for the last time. I went to her and said, "I'm sure whoever inherits this place, most likely his daughter, will keep it open and you'll still have your job."

"It feels like the end of an era. I guess it is with Del gone. Maybe she'll keep the place running, but that will be months and months away and by then everything will have changed. Max, I don't even know if I'd want to work here with a new boss. They're bound to make changes. I liked the routine. I knew where I stood. Does that make sense?"

"Absolutely. But sometimes change is good. Who knows what the future will bring, but hang in there, okay?"

"Okay."

A door banged shut from somewhere out the back and we both jumped a mile. Anxious barked, and raced around to the other side of the counter then through the doorway.

"Wait here." I sped after him, my heart hammering, adrenaline coursing, causing me to give chase even though it might be dangerous.

"Wait for me!" whispered Melody, although I wasn't sure why as Anxious was making a right racket, before she squeezed past me and ran the length of the corridor to the back door and flung it open.

Her shriek caused me to sprint and I charged through the doorway out into the alley, then stopped beside Melody and Anxious staring at a crouched figure right where Del had been murdered.

Chapter 6

"Bonnie?"

The woman turned from her crouched position, long dark hair falling over her face. She swiped it away almost angrily and looked up, her red-raw eyes filled with tears, streaks of mascara running down her cheeks. "Melody, is it true? It can't be."

"It's true. Someone murdered Del."

Bonnie stood, her stature at odds with her squat father, her frame very slim, so clearly not as into food as the rest of us. "Right here?"

"Yes, right here. I found him. It was awful."

"I… I don't understand. Who would do such a thing? Why? Everyone loved Dad. Good old Del from the deli. Always joking around with customers, never a cross word with anyone. Now he's gone? The police said I had to come to the station, or they'd send someone to speak to me, and I have to go to the morgue. The morgue! I had to come here first though. To see for myself. It's his blood, isn't it?"

We stared at the dark stain on the ground, the crime scene tape and chalk lines making the scene utterly surreal, so I couldn't imagine how it felt for Bonnie.

"Aunty Melody!" came a high-pitched call from two girls, clearly twins and clearly Del's grandchildren, as they raced out of the door. They must have been inside somewhere.

"Jane! Kim! How are you, girls?"

"Grampyd is dead!" wailed one of the twins, and then they both flung themselves at Melody and sobbed into her shoulder.

For just gone thirteen, they were almost as tall as Melody and their mother, and very slim, that awkward age where they were shooting up and had really long legs before the rest of their body caught up with the shock of puberty. However, their straight blond hair running all the way down their backs was in stark contrast to their mother's. Their pale complexions were blotchy because of their tears, but the similarity to Bonnie was still unmistakable. Button noses, full lips, and large eyes, although the girls' were blue rather than their mother's dark orbs. I couldn't help wondering what Bonnie's husband looked like, but I assumed he was blond and the genes had won out with the twins.

Bonnie joined her daughters and hugged both them and Melody, the women lost to their grief.

Anxious, and I have to admit, I, didn't know what to do, so we stood there, staring at the blood-soaked ground, waiting for them to recover.

Bonnie was the first to break free and the twins soon followed, and stood close to their mother, heads bowed, arms hanging straight by their sides. They were all shell-shocked by the news.

"Everyone, this is Max. Max, this is Bonnie, and her daughters, Jane and Kim. Don't ask me to tell you which one is which. I can never tell." Melody smiled at the girls, her love apparent.

"Stop teasing, Aunty Melody," said one, smiling, then her eyes welled.

"Hey, it's alright to smile, even after what's happened," said Bonnie, squeezing her daughter's shoulder. "Grampy would have wanted it that way." She turned to me and said, "Nice to meet you, Max. Sorry to ask, but who are you?"

"I'm afraid to say I was with Melody when she discovered your father. We've both been at the police station giving statements, then Melody was kind enough to show me the old airfield."

"He's a vanlifer," explained Melody.

"That's so cool," gushed one of the twins, glancing at me then looking away as if embarrassed. "I want to do that when I'm older. Apparently, us kids will never be able to afford a house anyway, so I'm gonna live in a van and make a YouTube channel and get rich."

"Everyone and their van are doing the same thing," said Melody, "so you better do it soon or there won't be any room left on YouTube."

"Silly Aunty, it can't run out of space."

"I suppose not." Melody hugged the girls again and I stroked Anxious who was trembling uncontrollably as he hadn't had a fuss yet and couldn't understand why not. Everyone adored him, so what was the hold up?

"I'm so sorry about Del. By the sounds of it, he was a great man."

Bonnie wiped her face and frowned at the make-up on her hands, then said, "He really was. I can't believe he's gone. I've been in this shop more times than I have my own home. Ever since I was a girl and we lived upstairs. He's always been here, and now he's gone. It doesn't feel real."

"Poor Grampy," said a twin.

"We loved him so much. Was it terrible? What did the police say? Have they caught the killer? What happened?"

"Wow, so many questions. But before I try to answer, would you mind giving the little guy a head rub or a pat or something? He's about to explode. He's not used to being ignored." I figured it might take their minds off things for a moment, plus, I didn't want an exploding dog. Things were messy enough already.

Anxious yipped his agreement, and everyone focused on him. The twins and Bonnie said how cute he was and bent to make a fuss of him, apologising that they hadn't even noticed him as they were so upset. Anxious soaked up the adoration in his usual style by prancing around and making an exhibition of himself then leaning into the head rubs and ear scratches, until finally it was over and we stood around, nobody knowing quite what to say.

"Let me try to answer some of your questions. Is it Jane or Kim?" I asked the girl who'd spoken to me.

"I'm Jane. You can tell because I have lighter blue eyes than Kim and am the pretty one."

"Are not!"

I laughed and said, "Ah, so you're the funny one as well as the prettiest?"

"She is not!"

"No, I think you're right, Kim. You are so much prettier."

"See?" crowed Kim, poking her tongue out at her sister.

"Do you really think so?" asked Jane, pouting.

"I do not. I think you are both incredibly pretty. You take after your mother, of course." I winked at Bonnie, who smiled and mouthed a silent, "Thank you," because the twins had forgotten about the terrible news for a while.

Melody nodded at me, then turned to the twins and suggested, "Girls, why don't you go upstairs and watch TV? I know you have the day off school because of the issue they had with the plumbing, so let us talk for a while then we'll come up to see you. Is that okay, Bonnie?"

"Yes, of course. That's a great idea. You don't want to be standing around here where…"

All eyes turned to the blood stain. Bonnie hugged the girls, then they went over to Melody and had a cuddle, and they even gave me and Anxious a hug too before they hurried off, talking quietly to each other.

"They're great kids," I told Bonnie. "You must be so proud."

"Like you wouldn't believe. Don't get me wrong, they're a right handful at times, but I wouldn't have it any other way. Max, I'm sorry to ask, but why on earth are you here? Melody, should you be inviting strangers into Dad's home? It doesn't feel right. No offence, Max, but this is the family home."

"I understand. Sorry to intrude, but I'm assuming the police haven't told you everything yet?"

Melody moved closer to Bonnie and said, "There's still a lot you don't know, so we better explain."

"I think you better. I have to go to the station soon, as I promised, not that I'm ready to face it yet, so what's going on?"

It didn't take too long to fill Bonnie in on the note and the peculiar circumstances of Del's murder, not that murder was ever normal. She listened without interrupting, allowing us to explain in detail, trying not to miss anything out.

"That doesn't sound like something Dad would do. He never left the shop unlocked until it was opening time. He always complained about people waiting outside before he opened, you know that, Melody, but he was a stickler for routine. Up at the crack of dawn, actually before, went to get his paper every morning, had a chat in the newsagents, then he'd be back at work and you always came at eight. It's always been that way. Tradition."

"That's what I told Max. Del liked his routine."

"And the note asked for you to look into this, Max? And that the knife was to be looked after? Was it his?"

"The police seem to think so. For a while they thought it was mine, as I have the same brand, but they checked my van while I was at the station and the complete set is there. They're very good knives. He liked quality, same as me."

"That's good to know," she laughed nervously, "as I'd hate to think you were the killer and were toying with us."

"He's a good guy, Bonnie," said Melody. "Max is kind of an amateur detective. He's going to look into this. We think that's why Del asked for him. He must have known about Max's skills and somehow he knew he would come to the shop."

"Wait, I don't get it. How could Dad have known? Max, did you speak to him? Email or something?"

"No, nothing like that. I came on a total whim. I had no plans to come here and had never heard of the place. I happened to find the door unlocked, so assumed the shop was open."

"This is crazy. It makes absolutely no sense whatsoever." Bonnie pulled her straight hair behind her ears and brushed out her fringe, then squeezed her lips tightly with her fingers, clearly very upset and stressed, and scared too. I was a stranger, somehow tied up in her father's murder, so I understood completely.

"I'm so sorry to unnerve you. Please don't be scared. I honestly want to help. Melody, maybe explain who I am? I'm not being big-headed, you understand, but I might be able to help figure this out. I have to. My name was on your father's note, and he asked for me. He even knew where I was staying, which I don't understand at all."

"Max, I'm not scared of you," said Bonnie. "Of course you want to help. If for no other reason than to clear your name. I'm sure the police weren't happy about this. You're a suspect. Or were. But if Dad asked for you, then he had his reasons. How on earth did he know where you were or when you'd arrive at the shop?"

"Guys, you're missing the obvious. It's social media. Max, I'm guessing you aren't a big online user?"

"Not really. Never been my thing. Or, it was, then I stopped. I don't have a signal half the time, so never bother with much beyond email or checking where I'm going to stay next. I have a few apps for that, but that's about it."

"There you go then. I've already found a few sites talking about you, and it seems like you have quite a following. People talking about your cases, discussing how you figured out the mysteries, that sort of thing. Bonnie, let me show you Max's wiki page so you know he's a genuine guy."

They spent a few minutes going over it, much to my discomfort, glancing up at me every so often. I felt like an insect under a microscope, and kept smiling self-consciously. Then they must have begun looking at the other stuff, forums, and whatnot, and soon became embroiled in it. Such things were a rabbit hole I never wanted to go down, and disliked that people were discussing my life in such detail. I supposed there was no escaping it in the modern age, but it left me feeling uneasy. They finished soon enough, and stood, gawping, like I was from another planet."

"Why are you staring?"

Melody turned to Bonnie and explained, "Max is one of those guys who doesn't realise he's a looker. I mean, look at him. Six one, lovely hair, the beard's a bit much, but he could cut it, and he clearly works out. He even has a tan and it's only March."

"He is very handsome. Modest too."

"Um, I am here, you know. Min always says I'm good looking, but I think she's biased."

"That's the ex-wife your father talks about on your wiki page?" asked Bonnie.

"Yes. She often visits, and we've solved quite a few mysteries together."

"Then she's a lucky woman. Max, haven't you seen what they're saying about you online?"

"No, I haven't. Like I said, it isn't my thing. I don't search for my own name. That would be weird, wouldn't it?"

"Everyone does it," said Melody. "Just in case anyone's saying something bad, or nice, about you."

"And what if they were? What could you do about it?" I wondered.

They exchanged a look, then Bonnie said, "You're right. There's nothing you could do. We still look anyway. But that's besides the point. Max, you've built up quite a following. People talk about you in forums and in chat rooms, and on all kinds of social media platforms. You're kinda famous. Not mega famous, but people follow along with your cases and even make videos about them. You should see the comments sections."

"I don't think I want to. So, we're good? I can look into this?"

"I would appreciate that. I'm sorry, but I better go. I'll get the girls."

"Leave them here," said Melody. "I'll watch them."

"Are you sure? That would be a help." She turned to me and explained, "My husband is at work, and I haven't even told him yet. He isn't answering, so must be somewhere without a signal. He's a mobile mechanic and often doesn't get reception. It's not exactly 5G around here."

"I'm sure he'll get the message soon enough. Would you like me to drive you to the station? I don't mind."

"That's kind, Max, but I'm fine to drive. It will give me a few minutes to get my head straight. It still doesn't feel real. Like a dream. Dad's really gone. For good. This place holds so many memories, and now I'll never see him again." Bonnie wandered off in a daze without saying goodbye.

"The poor thing," said Melody. "She was close with Del. She grew up here, and the twins love coming to visit their Grampy. He doted on those girls. They come every Saturday and help out. Mind you, that mostly means them getting in my way and making everything take twice and long, but it's sweet that they want to spend their Saturdays here."

"They seem like lovely kids. What about Bonnie's mum? Del's wife? She still around?"

"She wasn't the nicest woman. It was a long time ago that they split up, and I don't think Bonnie has heard from her in years. They weren't a happy family in the end, from what Del told me. I've never discussed it much with Bonnie. We aren't super close or anything like I was with Del. She wasn't a good mother, or wife, and the split wasn't amicable. She upped and left and hardly ever saw Bonnie again. She tried to have a relationship with her mum years afterwards, but it fell apart eventually and I don't think anyone even knows where she lives now. It's been years without contact."

"So she could be a suspect? Would she kill him?"

"I honestly don't know her. It was before my time here. More than twenty years ago. Del always said he wasn't a happy man until the day she left, and although it was traumatic for Bonnie, it was for the best."

"I wonder if the police will be able to track her down, or if Bonnie has heard from her?"

"We can ask her later. She'll be back after she's sorted out things. Right now, we need to see if we can find anything that can help. The girls will be alright for a while, so let's search, then we can check on them, and then we need to figure out what to do with all the food."

"Then we better get to it."

We checked the alley, even going through the bins, although the police had already done that. Nothing of interest was found, just the usual rubbish a busy deli would produce, and inside was no different. Every square inch had been gone over by the police and the various teams, and they'd taken anything they thought might be of interest away, not that there was much beyond the computer and some paperwork.

What I hadn't anticipated was how incredible Del's kitchen was. It was a chef's paradise. The room was spotless, so he'd obviously finished his cooking well before he was killed. Absolutely nothing was out of place and he'd even done the dishes. Knives were arranged neatly, the pots and pans the same, and everything seemed to have a place.

Melody explained that Del was a true perfectionist and by the time she arrived for work he'd quite often already finished in the kitchen, with little left for her to do but help to take everything out to the shop. She said that most deliveries happened around six in the morning, including bread and a few other very local offerings, with much of the rest being made by Del himself every morning or at least two to three times a week.

I could have spent hours in there drooling over the setup, but we had to check on the girls, then Melody promised to show me around town so we could chat to those who might have seen Del that morning. I didn't doubt that the DIs had already spoken to whoever they could, but often people told a different tale to a friendly face rather than the authorities, so it was worth pursuing.

Chapter 7

"Has Del always lived here?" I asked as we stood at the bottom of the stairs and looked up towards his flat above the shop.

"Ever since he bought the place with his wife way back when. Apparently, it was a nightmare when they separated as she wanted half of the business, or more like it, the sale of the premises. From what I learned over the years, it seems like everything turned nasty with the divorce as Del had to prove she'd never lifted a finger to help with the shop, and that he'd bought it with his own money. It ended up nearly bankrupting him anyway, and it took years for him to recover after he paid her off just to be done with it. He wanted a clean break and for her to be gone from their lives for good."

"But he held on to the place?"

"Yes. It was his life, Max. He lived here with Bonnie until she left for university, then she came back for a few years before moving out when she got hitched and had the twins. Del never wanted to move into a house and rent out the flat as it was so convenient for work. He lived for this place. It was what defined him."

"But it didn't make him lose touch with what was important? His family? That was the mistake I made when I was obsessed with my job. I neglected everything else."

"Del was different to that. Yes, he worked incredibly hard, but he knew how to find a balance. He was up at stupid o'clock every morning, and went to bed very early. But he also had a nap every afternoon, and he always took Sundays off. He'd visit Bonnie and the children. They usually had Sunday dinner together at hers, or he'd go for a walk or chill and read a book. He enjoyed his life."

"So what went wrong? What possible motive is there for killing him? Maybe it was the ex-wife? Maybe she's back on the scene?"

"I don't think so. Neither him nor Bonnie mentioned it, and trust me, I know, I mean knew, everything that went on in their lives. If it wasn't Del gossiping, it was Bonnie. Like I said, we aren't super close. We don't see each other outside of this place, but we chat for hours every week as she's always popping in and out. She doesn't have a regular job, as the girls and the house are more than a full-time commitment, but she comes around most days, and always with the kids on the weekend."

"Then we have our work cut out for us. Maybe we'll find something upstairs that will help us to figure this out."

"Let's hope so, as so far we have nothing to go on."

The stairs had new carpet, and were soft underfoot, and at the top I took a moment to enjoy the simplicity of the spacious landing where various doors led off to the rooms. The house was deep, very deceiving from outside, so he had what amounted to a generous sized bungalow up here. Del was clearly a man who liked a comfortable, plain home with a few modern touches but plenty of rather old-fashioned furniture too. He wasn't the kind of man to be spending hours perusing shops for new items, but what he did have he looked after.

The carpet matched the stairs throughout, and Melody explained it had all been done last year as it hadn't been replaced for decades. The bedrooms were plain, but nice, but there wasn't anything of note in either Del's or the spare room that was once Bonnie's. Now it was just a storage room, and evidently a place to keep toys for the twins that they'd mostly grown out of over the years, but Del couldn't bear to part with.

The kitchen was modern, but in a plain grey with matching countertop, and the bathroom was the usual bachelor style with the distinct lack of a feminine touch, but clearly suited his needs. All that remained to investigate was the living room, which we'd left to last so we could snoop around without disturbing the youngsters. They'd been very quiet so far, with just the occasional murmur or quick laugh before they talked quietly or bickered over what to watch next.

It was so different for children nowadays, with not only endless channels to choose from, but endless videos on the various social media platforms. Not to mention Youtube, where hours could be lost scrolling through video shorts before you came up for air and realised you'd wasted half a day without even finding what you'd been looking for. You'd somehow managed to spend hours learning how to solder, or repair a broken gutter, even though you'd begun by searching for something totally unrelated.

As we poked our heads into the living room, it was to find the girls doing exactly that. Scrolling through endless short clips on Youtube, eyes locked to the TV screen, sitting no more than three feet away. They were holding hands and very close, sometimes whispering to each other about what they were watching, but it was obvious their attention kept wavering, and their upset was palpable. They missed their Grampy, and now and then their eyes would drift to the various ornaments or an old striped recliner that was clearly where he sat of an evening or possibly to nap.

We loitered in the doorway, not wanting to disturb the girls, as without discussing it Melody and I both knew that the moment we entered and they became aware of us, their thoughts would inevitably return to what had happened. I took the time to study the room closely, noting the old sideboard with a few generic ornaments mixed with what must have been things the twins had made for him when younger. Several photos took pride of place on the mantle, but apart from a few lamps and the clearly new black leather sofa, there wasn't much else to even indicate who had lived here. Del was a man after my own heart, as he'd kept things sparse for ease of cleaning and to maximise whatever free time he had.

"Hey, girls, how are you doing?" asked Melody.

They turned and jumped even at the soft words, and Jane flicked off the TV like they'd been caught being naughty.

"We're okay," she said.

They clearly weren't, as their cheeks were red, their eyes moist, and their lips were trembling. They were holding it together, but only just.

"Have you found anything out?" asked Kim, squeezing her sister's hand tighter.

"Not yet," I said, "but that doesn't mean we won't. Is there something you'd like to tell us?"

They exchanged a glance, then shook their heads, their long hair bouncing. Each wiped the other's eyes, then they held my gaze for a flicker of their eyelids and smiled weakly.

"If there is, then it might help," encouraged Melody. "Maybe someone you saw, something you heard. Anything?"

"Like what?" asked Jane.

"We aren't sure." I noted how their eyes never stayed still, constantly roaming from me to Melody, then off into empty space. I wondered if they were always nervy like this or it was because of the terrible incident. "Maybe you overheard a conversation or maybe you saw someone you didn't recognise. Maybe Del told you something in private, but now you think back it seems strange. When did you last speak to him?"

"Yesterday, when he came over for dinner. He always comes on Sunday. He was joking around like always. He was in a good mood, right, Kim?"

"Really upbeat. He always loved Sundays. It was his day off. And we were in the shop on Saturday. Mum went off to do some shopping and we helped Melody, didn't we?"

"You sure did. And you earned every penny of your wages."

"You get paid for working here?"

"Grampy used to give us a few pound every week when we were little. But now we're older he made it official and we're proper employees. We work hard, don't we, Aunty?"

"You sure do. And it means you have some proper money to buy your own things with." Melody turned to me and explained, "They like to buy clothes sometimes, or go to the cinema."

"It's great that you have jobs. Gives you some independence. Did anyone come in on Saturday and act strange? Anything out-of-the-ordinary at all?"

"Nothing," said Kim. "Just another day. We joked around with Grampy, and had fun with Melody, and that was it."

"Thanks, girls, you've been a great help," said Melody.

"No, we haven't! We haven't done anything!" Jane burst into tears and Kim followed, then they hugged each other and their shoulders racked as they sobbed.

Anxious whimpered, then crept forward. He was a sensitive soul and hated for anyone to be upset, and knew that he could help. He pawed at each girl's arm gently, mindful of their bare skin, and when they glanced up he whined softly, distracting them. It had the desired effect and they focused on him, and when he rolled over, let his legs flop open, and exposed his tummy, they were unable to resist rubbing his stomach and laughing as his tongue lolled and his tail swished back and forth.

"What did you like to do with Del the most?" I asked to further distract them.

"We liked playing all kinds of games with him. And we watched quite a few Youtube videos too. Stuff about camping and vanlife and things like that."

"They don't want to hear about that," chastised Kim, nudging Jane.

Jane reddened, then hung her head, and said, "Sorry. Um, we liked mysteries too."

"Jane, that isn't helping," warned Kim again.

"Then what will? He's dead!"

"Why don't you go and fix yourselves a drink?" suggested Melody. "There're fizzy drinks in the fridge. Maybe stick the kettle on for me and Max?"

Numbly, they nodded, then stood, but didn't leave the room.

"What is it?" I asked.

"We were just wondering. What's it like to be a vanlifer? Is it really cool? Everyone in school is so into it and it looks awesome."

"Ah, you said you wanted to get a van when you were older, didn't you?" I asked Jane.

"Yeah, it seems amazing! Travelling, and meeting all kinds of people, and doing your own thing. Grampy loved hearing about what we'd do when we get our van."

"He did? I thought he liked being here?"

"Sure he did. He loved this place. But he liked the idea of travelling too. Guess sometimes he wondered what it would be like to not have a business and be free."

"Then I'll tell you. Sometimes it's amazing, and lots of fun. But it gets cold and damp, and it's annoying having to find laundrettes and use public toilets and not always have a shower when you want one. But seeing so many amazing places, and, like you said, being free, makes up for all that."

"You're so cool," mumbled Kim, reddening.

"Thank you. That's very kind."

They shuffled past, heads down, then went into the kitchen.

As Anxious rolled over, he must have hit the remote control as the TV turned back on. As he moved, the dropdown menu on the TV was shown with a list of videos in the history. I gasped as I pointed to the TV, and told Melody, "There are videos about me. Look."

"Max, I told you, you're all over social media. People are discussing your murder mysteries. Some make videos and try to figure out how you solved them."

"But why are they on Del's TV? It means he knew about me, doesn't it? That maybe he's been following me?"

"Let's take a look."

Melody retrieved the remote and Anxious immediately curled up in her lap as she sat, so we flicked through the most recent things that'd been watched. Most were weird videos with girls giving fashion advice, but going back over a few weeks they were interspersed with various ones where the presenters discussed my escapades and others mostly about vanlife in general but using my name, possibly as clickbait.

Del had clearly been following my life, much like he had on his computer where he'd searched for any mention of me online. It was weird and disconcerting to discover how many people were talking about me and the interest I'd garnered, and when it came to the comments sections I was gobsmacked.

Melody turned it off after we'd gone through the listings, then faced me and said, "Told you people were obsessed."

"I kinda get it, although I don't like it. But how come Del was interested? He ran a deli but was looking for any mention of me. Why?"

"Maybe he and the girls did it together. They're into the vanlife. A lot of young kids are, even though they can't drive. It's the appeal of being able to travel without it costing a fortune, and tiny houses are a massive thing now. All the youngsters know house prices are ridiculous, so they start talking about building their own, or getting vans. Families with large plots are building tiny homes for children as it literally costs the same as a few years' rent."

"But they're thirteen. Did you think about houses and stuff at that age?"

"Absolutely not, but we didn't have the internet like they do now when I was a kid. It's different for them, Max.

They go down a rabbit hole and end up focusing on something for a while before they move on to the next thing. It's just how it is." Melody shrugged; this was how modern life worked.

"Maybe the girls did watch this stuff with Del."

At that moment, they returned with their drinks. "Kettle's boiled. Want me to make coffees?" asked Kim.

"We'll do it in a minute, thanks. Did you know about Max before today? Before he turned up, I mean?"

"Us?" asked Kim. "Why?"

"Just wondered if you'd heard his name or seen Del looking him up?"

"We heard about you from friends, how you solved these murders, but we never knew your name before the other week. Maybe we told Grampy we'd heard what you did, but we never watched or looked anything up with him. Why?"

"Oh, nothing, just trying to get a clear picture of everything. Right, we've got stuff to do in the shop. Will you be alright up here until your mum returns? She won't be too long."

They nodded, so I called for Anxious and after making coffee we returned to the shop to see what we could do with the food, and to discuss things further.

"Are they always so jittery, or is it because of what's happened?"

"They're normally more confident, sure, but that might be because you're here. They don't know you."

"What about this talk of Del and vanlife? He ever discuss it with you?"

"Never. It's the first I've heard of it. I know the girls have been excited about it lately, but they go through so many different interests it's hard to keep up. A month ago, they were raving about being airline stewards so they could travel the world, and were obsessed with watching videos. Before that there was a phase about clothes, and some TV show, and there's always their changing music tastes. It's just youngsters getting excited by stuff."

"So Del never said a thing about maybe wanting to close the shop and doing something different? Travel maybe?"

"Max, if you knew him, you'd know he would never do that. I'm guessing he was humouring the girls. Although, it is weird he was watching videos. Maybe he was checking out vanlife to be able to talk about it with them. That's probably how he came across your name."

"I guess. But it still doesn't explain how he knew where I was or when I'd arrive. Melody, I have to admit, it's freaking me out. I had a stalker in the past, and although it was resolved and wasn't anything to worry about, it got weird later on. This has me rattled."

"Max, I'm sure it's nothing. I don't know how he knew where you'd be, but maybe someone spotted you and posted it online and he just happened to see it."

"But there was nothing like that when I looked at his computer. Nothing that recent."

"Then we better get busy figuring this out. First, we need to decide what to do with the food."

"Then I have the obvious answer. But won't it be weird to empty the shop of so much? It will look very different."

"Anything is better than it going to waste, and you heard Bonnie. She said Del would hate for it to be ruined and better an empty shop than a mouldy one."

"That's true. Then why don't we see if there are any charities that would want it? Are they any homeless shelters, or needy causes where the grub would be welcomed?"

"Around here? Are you kidding? Of course there are! Why didn't I think of that?"

"Because you've got other things on your mind. Why don't you make a few calls, and I'll begin packing everything away so it won't spoil? We can take it to wherever you think is best."

"Great idea."

While Melody wandered around with her phone glued to her ear, I hunted around in the back rooms for suitable boxes and containers, then began to sort through everything that would most likely have sold by now, and carefully packed it ready to give to those in need. Certain foodstuffs would keep for a few weeks so I loaded it into the large fridges, and even put some into the freezers, feeling sure that once this was over, Bonnie would be able to decide what to do with the shop, if it truly was her who'd inherit the business.

Melody found the perfect solution to the food issue, then helped to finish sorting things out. We performed a final sweep of the place but found no clues, and as we entered the shop again, Bonnie returned looking absolutely awful.

Chapter 8

"Is it too early for wine?" Bonnie almost crumpled right in the middle of the shop, but instead she smiled wanly, her arms limp by her sides, then turned in a circle slowly as if seeing the room for the first time. "It finally feels real. He's gone."

"Would you like a cuppa?" I offered. "Or wine if you weren't joking."

"Thank you, Max, but I'm okay. Wine isn't a smart idea, as if I start I don't think I'd stop. And I just had several cups of horrid police coffee, so I'll pass on a cuppa too. This place means so much to me, to all of us, and now it's done. What am I going to do, Melody?"

"You'll get through it. You're a tough woman and Del wouldn't like to see you this way. Be strong."

"Yes, you're right. I will be strong. For me, for the girls, and for Dad. He always said he put this place in my name, and that if anything happened I'd inherit it, but what am I going to do with it anyway? And it has to shut until the paperwork is sorted. Melody, I'm so sorry, and I know how much the shop means to you. I'll be sure to keep paying your wages, and hopefully in a few weeks we'll know what to do."

"You don't have to do that. You can't afford it."

"It will come from the inheritance. I won't have you go without just because a maniac killed my dad. What should we do once we know where we stand? I can't imagine ever selling. That's not what Dad wanted, especially if it got turned into something else."

"Don't worry about that now. Focus on getting through the next few days and giving Del a proper send-off. That's what he would have wanted. All the rest can wait."

"Yes, you're right. Of course. Gosh, what a day."

While Melody and Bonnie embraced, and Bonnie sobbed quietly into Melody's shoulder, I finalised the packing. When I'd done, both women were standing stock still and staring at the now empty display cabinets.

"Sorry it looks so different. I know it's not how things should be, but better than it going to waste."

"It's what Dad would have been happy with. He hated anything being wasted and always ensured he only made as much as he could sell. It's why people came early. By mid-afternoon, he always sold out of the daily perishables. It looks so different though. So… so final."

"I thought we could take the food to the food bank. They're more popular than ever these last few years. Everyone's struggling, and so many people need a little help, so what do you think? I called and they said they'd be really grateful, but if you don't think it's the best idea I'm open to suggestions." Melody smiled at Bonnie, whose eyes were unfocused, and I wasn't sure she was even listening.

"Yes, absolutely! That's a sweet idea. Sorry, I'm just shell-shocked from talking to the detectives. They were kind, and very understanding, but they had endless questions. Then I had to identify Dad's body to make it official. He looked like a waxwork doll. For a moment, I thought it wasn't him. That it was a mannequin. But it was. It was him. He's gone." Bonnie shook her head, raven hair bouncing, then rubbed at her eyes, refusing to cry.

"Are you sure you won't have a drink?" asked Melody.

"No, I'm fine. Seriously, thank you both so much for watching the girls. Have they been okay? No trouble?"

"No trouble," said Melody.

"Good as gold," I agreed. "Bonnie, I know you're distraught, but do you mind if I ask you a question?"

"Not more questions," she chuckled, smiling but clearly utterly exhausted and drained by the terrible day.

"I know it's the last thing you want to do. I'll make it quick. The girls seem really into vanlife, and we noticed that Del had been watching various videos about van conversions but mostly about people travelling around the country. But what caught our eyes was that he'd seen a few videos of people discussing the cases I've been involved in. Did he ever mention any of that to you?"

"Just that he was humouring the girls. It's their latest thing. A phase like so many others. They watch some YouTube or the other platforms with short videos. They make it look so glamorous when I bet it's all muddy floors and trying to find somewhere to have a poo."

"True," I laughed. "So, the girls never mentioned me? They said they'd heard of me, that they are into vanlife but hadn't told Del. Maybe Del said something and you forgot, as why would you remember?"

"Max, it's so kind that you're willing to help, but honestly, no, I'd never heard of you. He didn't mention your name. I can't imagine Dad was watching stuff about travelling, but maybe he got caught up in it now and then when there was nothing on the TV. It was just to humour his grandchildren. He always tried to show an interest in whatever they are obsessed with at the moment. He was kind like that."

"That makes sense, and it's what Melody said too. Sorry to pester you. We'll go and deliver the food, and leave you in peace."

"I really appreciate this. Thank you both. Max, you're a stranger. Why are you being so kind?"

"Because Del sounds like a great man. We clearly both had an obsession with food, and I appreciate the work he did here. It's a true art. But let's not forget, he wrote me that message, and wanted me to solve his murder. That's incentive enough."

Bonnie nodded. "I'm still grateful. I'll close up the shop after you've gone, and take the girls home. I spoke to Tony, that's my husband, and he's on his way back to the house. The girls will be so pleased to see him. Thank you for everything you've done, and I'm sure we'll speak soon. For now, I just want to go home."

Bonnie left, walking like a zombie, and I was certain she'd fall apart the moment she saw her husband. She had too much pent-up emotion and it would boil over soon enough.

"The poor woman," I said once we heard movement upstairs.

"She's going to crash soon. Come on, let's get this food to those who need it. Then we can have a chat with people and find out if anything odd happened this morning." Melody grabbed a box, so I held the door open then took several more and we began loading up Vee. There was a works van, but I thought it best not to use it as it would only upset Melody more.

Anxious was in his element, nose almost glued to the various boxes we loaded, and he even managed to snaffle a few crumbs, and I got the sneaking suspicion possibly several pork pies too. Once everything was stacked up then lashed down with bungee cords to avoid any unfortunate accidents of the culinary kind that would see Anxious gorging until he popped, we headed off.

Melody was a strong woman, that much was obvious, and the more time I spent with her, the more it became apparent that she truly doted on Del. Considering she'd worked for him, it seemed rather unusual, as more often than not, the boss and staff relationship wasn't a close one. For nearly everyone in the country with a full-time job, they spent more time with work colleagues than their own families. It led to tension, resentment, and settled into merely doing what was needed to survive, but Melody and Del's relationship was clearly special. She was lucky to have had him in her life. Of course, being so close, the loss was that much greater, but she was a stalwart and would get through this.

"Do you think Bonnie will run the business?" I wondered.

"I don't see how she can. The girls are a full-time job at their age, and her husband works long, erratic hours. It's the nature of being on call all the time. He's up early and sometimes back very late. She has to be there for school runs, sorting out meals, not to mention running the house. I think this might be the end of it. I don't know what I'll do without the job, but I'll manage somehow."

"Maybe she'll keep it on. She seems to think an awful lot of you and the deli. And she wants to honour her dad's memory."

"Maybe. We'll see."

"Melody, don't take this the wrong way, and you know I'm only trying to help, but you don't suppose there's a chance that Bonnie…"

"Out with it, Max, although I already know what you're going to say."

"Could she have done it? Were they really very close?"

"They were super tight. Best friends, I suppose. It was just them for a long time, then the twins came along and they got closer again after Melody getting married and obviously not being around as much. She loved him, and I know there's an inheritance, but she would never, ever, hurt him, let alone murder him."

"Of course, but I had to ask. What about this Tony, her husband? Do they have money worries? You said he worked long hours. Maybe things are worse than you know."

"Nice bloke. A bit rough around the edges, like me, and not the type you'd think Bonnie would go for, but he's decent enough. He works hard to provide for his family, enjoys the job, actually, and they've been happily married since day one. Like I said, Bonnie and I aren't particularly close, but she tells me enough and Del loved to gossip. He never had a bad word to say about Tony. Dads are super protective of their little girls, and he was wary of Tony when they started dating as he's quite a handful, but since then he's had nothing but good things to say about him. No arguments, no breaks-ups, no trouble at all. They aren't strapped for cash either. He earns decent money."

"So he couldn't have done it?"

"Killed Del?" Melody turned to me, shocked, and shook her head, tutting. "Max, you've been around too much bad stuff. Not everyone's a killer, you know. Most people could never do that."

"I may have been around too many terrible crimes, but trust me, Melody, everyone has it in them. Sure, normally the killings are from someone who is unhinged, but they always seem normal enough until they confess. Given the right circumstances, anyone is capable of the most heinous crimes."

"Maybe, but not Tony. He's a good guy. And besides, why would he do it?"

"Money? Revenge for a perceived insult? An argument that got out of hand? Who knows?"

"If that was the case, how did Del know it was going to happen? That's not exactly a spur-of-the-moment crime if he knew it was coming."

"True."

"Hey, I just had an idea! Hear me out, as I know it sounds crazy, but what if, and I have no idea why, Del hired a hitman?"

"To have himself killed, you mean?"

"Sure. Is that wild?"

"Pretty wild. That sounds like something from a movie. Man hires hitman because he finds out he has a terminal disease, then changes his mind but it's too late and he has to try to stop the man he hired from doing the deed. Actually, I'm sure I did watch that movie."

With a grin, Melody admitted, "Um, I think I might have too! But it's possible, isn't it? Maybe he did have a terrible illness he was keeping from everyone and thought this was a way to avoid a nasty, slow death."

"There are a few problems with the theory. The main one being, he wasn't ill, was he?"

"Not that I know of, but Del wouldn't have said if he was. He'd have worked until he dropped."

"And the other issue is, where on earth would a hard-working deli owner find a hitman?"

"The Yellow Pages?" Melody laughed at her own joke, then added, "I guess there isn't even that massive book anymore. It's all online now."

"I think they still print them, but I haven't seen one in years. Let's dismiss that option as you were only joking, right?"

"Kind of. I'm trying to go through every possible option I can think of. There has to be an answer."

"And we'll find it, or the detectives will. We'll get to the truth eventually."

We remained silent for the rest of the short trip, the only sound the purring of Vee, seemingly happy to be performing a good deed, and the constant whimpering of Anxious who was belted into the back where he kept a morose eye on the boxes of food, inconsolable as he wasn't allowed to have at it.

When we parked and I opened the side door, I gave the desperately sad pooch a biscuit and he perked right up and lay down outside Vee while Melody and I ferried the first of the boxes to a community centre she explained was used as a food bank once a week.

We met a nice lady at the door, explained who we were, and she called for a few volunteers who made short work of the boxes while we had a chat with Veronica.

She explained that she'd been involved in the charity for years, but hadn't known the service to be in such demand until post-COVID. With the massive countrywide upheaval of jobs and so many businesses dissolving after the lockdowns, people were feeling the pinch like never before. Even years later, there was no sign of things improving for many, and the weekly free food was all that kept their heads above water.

"Who supplies the food?" I asked.

"We have various drop-off points at local shops, and some of the supermarkets allow us to have containers where people can pop in some of their shopping. We get a lot of contributions, and we're so grateful. People like Del are so generous. But I have to say, this is most unusual. We don't normally get such large donations from him. Maybe once or twice a week he'll drop off a few things, and it's nice to see you again, Melody, but what's happened?"

"You don't know?" I asked, shocked.

"Didn't I tell you?" asked Melody, looking flustered.

"Tell me what? Are you alright? What's happened?"

"Veronica, I'm sorry to tell you this, but Del's dead. He was murdered this morning. With a knife."

"What!? Poor Del. He was such a charming man, and so kind. I had a little crush on him, actually, and always wanted to say something. Now he's gone. Who would do such a thing?"

"That's what we'd like to know," said Melody. "I assumed everyone here would have heard. Everyone in town does."

"We've only just got here for the afternoon. A few of us sorting things out for later when everyone comes for the food. People have jobs, but they still can't make ends meet, so we moved it to the evenings so everyone gets their chance. But tell me more. What happened?"

Veronica was early sixties but a strong woman with serious heft, solid, but athletic, with a shock of unapologetic white hair that reminded me of Albert Einstein on a particularly bad hair day. She wore red lipstick and dark eye make-up, with a pink tracksuit and white Adidas trainers. Practical, and unfussy, just like her. I took to her immediately, as this was clearly a very kind-hearted, community focused lady who took her role as the leader of this charity very seriously.

Between us, we explained what had happened, who I was, but left out anything about the note as the detectives had requested it be kept private. Veronica comforted Melody, tutted a lot, and was dumbfounded when we explained where and when Del had been found. We put my involvement down to being the first on the scene and having been caught up in other such mysteries, and she accepted it, seemingly only half listening as she tried to keep an eye on the volunteers and the food, whilst keeping Melody wrapped in her impressive arms.

"What can I do to help? And thank you so much for thinking of us. Everyone will be feasting tonight. It means so much, and I'm sure Del would be grateful for the help."

"Can you keep your ears open and see what people are saying?" asked Melody, shifting back beside me. "It's not very likely the killer will pop over and spill the beans, but something might catch your attention."

"Of course. I still can't believe it, and I'm amazed I hadn't heard. Mind you, I haven't checked my phone all day as it's in the car, so maybe there are a hundred calls from people gossiping. I bet this evening will be carnage with everyone talking about it."

"Let me know if anything comes up," said Melody.

We checked everything was gone from the van, then I secured Anxious and we headed back towards town. Melody suggested I take a detour to the canal, so I went where she directed then pulled up in a dirt car park and she surprised me by getting into the back and bringing out a small box she'd tucked away.

"What's that?"

"What Del would have wanted. Max, you've done so much already today, so I figured we should have ourselves a treat. I kept some of the food for us, and Anxious, of course, so we can have a nice late picnic. I don't know about you, but I'm absolutely starving. A final farewell to Del. It's out of respect, you understand? He'd have wanted this."

When Melody opened up the box, my smile spread, Anxious woofed for joy, and we settled on a picnic bench beside the canal and watched swans drift by as I ate what had to be the best picnic lunch I'd ever had.

Del truly was a master of his art, and the world was a worse place for his passing.

Chapter 9

After letting our delayed lunch settle, but not for too long as otherwise it would be getting late to talk to everyone, we reluctantly returned to Vee and loaded what little food was left into the fridge before I drove the short distance back into town.

The lights were off at the deli, a sad sign of things to come, and Melody was understandably upset, but she put a brave face on things and gave me a potted history of how Del's morning routine worked.

Every working day, Saturdays included, come rain or come shine, was the same. He would be up by four, work for an hour or so in the kitchen, go out for his paper, then stop and chat to the milkman, which I was astonished to hear was still doing the rounds in Welshpool, and have a quick chat with a few other local characters. Melody knew his route off by heart, and exactly who he spoke to every morning. Del loved to gossip, so would always recount with relish any juicy details he uncovered.

We decided to start at the newsagents.

"Okay, so let me fill you in quickly." Melody slowed, then stopped a few shops away outside a kebab place. "Sam, the owner, is a cranky so-and-so who's run the shop for as long as I can remember. He grew up in the flat upstairs, inherited the business when his dad retired, and lives and breathes the place. He opens at five thirty in the morning, closes at nine at night, and you can guarantee that whenever you go in, he'll be there."

"Those are crazy long hours."

"I know. He has two members of staff, part-timers, but he insists on being around anyway."

"And he's the one who opens up every morning?"

"Every single morning. Even Sundays. It's hard to believe, but plenty of people still like their morning paper. Sam has a paperboy to make deliveries, but mostly it's people who stop on the way to work or those who are up early and take a stroll and have a natter with him. On Sundays, it's crazy busy for the big papers with all the magazines and whatnot, but there's no money to be made from any of that."

"What's the main earner for him them?"

"You seriously need to ask?" Melody frowned at me and waited, but I just shrugged.

"Max, the same as how all newsagents, not that they should be called that now, make their money. Booze, smokes, and overpriced baked beans, sugar, milk, and other essentials people can't do without."

"Oh, right."

"Wow, you really are out of the loop in some regards, aren't you?"

"I guess I am," I laughed. "Let's go and say hi."

Melody sniggered, which wasn't a good sign, then pushed on the door. The usual annoying buzzer went, and yet again I wondered how anyone could stand the noise going off hundreds of times a day. It would drive me mad! I followed on her heels, keen to get inside, as the temperature was dropping and I was absolutely not dressed for the cold.

As the door swung shut, I stopped and gasped, then rubbed my eyes. Anxious whined, then sat and faced the door, the sensory overload too much for him. I let him back out and asked him to wait, and wished I could stay, too, but I simply had to look.

The shop was absolutely rammed with all manner of goods. Shelves and racking covered every available surface, from floor to ceiling, with more freestanding units running in parallel left to right. The counter was up against the right-hand wall behind the window, with shelves stocked with spirits, a shuttered cabinet I knew would house tobacco, but a colourful display of e-cig liquid screamed at me.

Newspapers were bundled on the floor by the door, presumably ones that didn't sell and would be collected for return, but magazines took up one entire section of wall. Everywhere else was dedicated to endless tinned goods, along with large freezers, fridges, an array of household cleaning products, and random displays of toys, even work boots and a bizarre stack of washing-up bowls almost to the ceiling. I couldn't even begin to understand how you'd find anything, but I guess this was a local shop for local people, so they knew what was what.

Close to freaking out as my OCD couldn't handle the riot of colours, the seeming lack of order, the fact baked beans were next to Marigolds, I turned to the corner and smiled at the young man as he caught my eye. He nodded, but looked beyond bored, and didn't return the smile and just continued staring at his phone.

"Paulie, I told you to stop looking at that damn phone!" a man, I presumed Sam, boomed as he marched across the shop floor, more like squeezed between the aisles even though he was very slim, and banged a fist on the counter on the tiny amount of space not taken up with the chocolate display.

"Sam, it was just to check a message," whined the young man.

"Liar! All you do is watch nonsense and avoid doing your work. If you aren't serving, you should be stacking or sweeping. I've told you a million times." Sam sighed dramatically, then turned to us. When he saw Melody, his features softened and he ran a hand over his liver-spotted head, tugging at the few hairs that remained. He reached out with long fingers, the skin as wrinkled as his pale face, and said, "Oh, Melody. Terrible news. Absolutely terrible. How are you, girl? Are you coping? Do you need anything? Anything at all? What can I do to ease your pain? I saw Bonnie earlier and the poor thing was beside herself. What are we going to do without Del? He was such a great man. The best."

"Thanks, Sam. Yes, it's terrible news. Thank you for the kind words."

"Those poor children. Imagine losing your grandfather like that. They must be heartbroken."

"They're pretty cut up, but you know what children are like. They're coping, and will bounce back."

"I'm sure they will, but it will take time. They doted on Del. Every Saturday morning without fail they'd be in here at half eight to buy some sweets. They were always nattering about the shop. Lovely girls. Sweet as pie. Mind you, they seemed distracted the last time they came in."

"How so?" I asked. "I'm Max, by the way."

"Max, nice to meet you." Sam shook my hand, his grip astonishingly strong, although he wasn't one of those men who tried to prove their manliness by gripping tighter than was needed; he was just a powerful guy.

"You too."

"And how do you two know each other? Finally got yourself a guy, have you?" he asked Melody with a cheeky wink.

"It isn't like that," snapped Melody. "Sorry, I'm still on edge. Max was there when we found Del. Me and him. He just wanted to buy some food, but the door was open when it shouldn't have been and—"

"Open? Del was a stickler for the rules. He never left the door open early." Sam scratched at his bald head, a deep frown creasing his brow. "What else happened? I've heard some of it, you know what people are like for gossiping, but you better tell me everything."

"We will, Sam, but first, what's this about the girls acting strangely?"

"Oh, nothing. The usual kid stuff, I assume. When they came in on Saturday, like always, they weren't their chatty selves. I asked them what was wrong, but they went quiet. Once they picked their sweets and came to the counter, they'd brightened a bit, the lure of sugar, I suppose, so I asked them again if everything was alright."

"And what did they say?"

"That they were planning a big adventure. That they were going to go travelling in a van or some such nonsense."

"They said they were going to go? That it was planned?"

"Who knows? They were whispering to each other a lot. They always do that. I guess it's a twins thing. I asked them what they meant, and told them they were never to go off with strangers, but they sniggered and said it wasn't like that. That they were going to be vanlifers with Del. That's it, I guess."

"They didn't say anything else?" asked Melody.

"Just the usual about sweets. I gave them a few extra treats for free as they're good girls, then they were on their way. Why are you so interested? What aren't you telling me?"

"Sam, Max here is a vanlifer, and he happened to be in the shop this morning, so when we heard about the girls talking about vans we just wondered is all."

"That's a mighty coincidence, isn't it?"

"Seems like that's all it is," I said, trying to steer the conversation away before Melody accidentally talked about Del's message to me. "Sam, how did Del seem this morning? Anything unusual? What did you talk about?"

Sam glanced at the door as the buzzer went and smiled at the young man who entered, then nodded to the lad behind the counter to get busy, so he served while we moved deeper into the shop, my OCD screaming at me to move the washing up liquid away from the tinned tomatoes, but I managed to hold it together.

"It was just the regular banter. Del seemed fine. You know Del, he didn't like to complain. In fact, he never did. Usually."

"Usually?" asked Melody, shooting a glance my way.

"It was kind of strange now I come to think of it. Should I be telling you this, or the police? They've already been around, you know. Two very strange detectives. Cagney and Lacy they were not. Anyway, where was I?"

"Del was acting a little strange?"

"Yes, that's right! He seemed tired, or more tired than usual. Mondays are his best days, after Sunday resting, but this morning he seemed exhausted. Said he was up late planning for something, but didn't say what. He was distracted, and kept muttering about hoping he didn't get into trouble. I asked him what he meant, but he laughed and dismissed it, waving his hands around like he always did."

"He did like to use his hands a lot," agreed Melody, encouraging Sam to continue.

"He sure did. I've lost count of the amount of things he's knocked over in here." Sam chuckled, eyes drifting, keeping an eye on customers as they squeezed along the groaning aisles. "So, he said it was no big deal, just an exciting thing he had coming up. He didn't elaborate, and you know how it gets in here in the mornings. Everyone's in a hurry, wanting to be served quickly so they can get to work."

"Anything else? No names mentioned or exactly what was going on?"

"That was it. He wasn't his usual self, but I think he'd been up late watching the TV."

"What gives you that idea?" I asked.

"He was muttering about wishing he hadn't started looking at travel videos with the twins. Laughed it off, saying he didn't know how the kids coped with so much entertainment all the time. That nobody could switch off anymore. I think he'd been up past his usual early bedtime and that's why he was out of sorts. Look, I'm sorry, but I have to go. That fool I have working here is what I'm talking about. Always on his phone scrolling through whatever nonsense the kids watch these days. He can't focus for more than a few seconds before getting distracted."

With a nod, we manoeuvred around the displays and left while Sam shouted at the lad who kept glancing at his phone.

Bending to Anxious, I told him, "You were lucky you waited outside. You'd have gone crazy in there. Sam had the tinned sweetcorn next to baby wipes."

Anxious gasped, then shook his head, as if to agree that he had a lucky escape.

"Do you really think he understands you?" asked Melody, looking strangely serious.

"Don't worry, I'm not a nutter. And of course he does. Mostly. Um, some of the time. If it involves the S word."

"Sausages, you mean?"

"No, don't say it!"

"Oops." Melody giggled as Anxious ran circles around us, keening for the pork-based delight no dog could ever get enough of but Anxious would now have to forego unless we got ones without all the bad stuff in.

"Come on, Anxious, we have other people to visit. Maybe you can have a chat with a few of them, too, this time." I winked at Melody, who stifled a giggle, her spirits lifted. I asked her, "Who's next?"

"May as well grab Charlie. He's the milkman."

"You said about that earlier. There's really still a milkman? With a milk float and everything?"

"Sure there is. Why?"

"Because it's not something you see any more. I don't know when I last saw milk being delivered."

"It's still common around here. Not to all the houses, but the shops and a few locals in town still get daily deliveries. There's a farm up the road that supplies it, so it's properly local. No supermarket stuff, but proper milk.

Charlie was one of the first people to drive an electric vehicle. Did you know that?"

"I guess the milk floats were the first electric vehicles in the country. I hadn't thought about that before."

"Then let's go have a chat with him."

"Won't he have finished by now? Surely he starts early?"

"Of course he's finished. He completes his rounds before the shops even open. How else could people have their milk for cereal?"

Melody gave me a funny look, so I smiled and said, "Of course. How silly of me."

"There you go then. Charlie goes home, has a kip, then comes back into town in the afternoon for a pint. Or maybe three. Sometimes four." Melody winked, then giggled as she punched me playfully on the arm.

"Every day?" I asked, dubious.

"Apart from Sundays. He goes to his daughter's for Sunday roast. Like Del, and plenty of others around here, he's a man of routine. I think you're the same, even though you travel a lot. I could tell when you were setting up your kitchen under the gazebo."

"I do like things done a certain way," I admitted.

"There you go then! Come on, it's a nice day still, although a bit nippy for shorts and a vest, Max. And hasn't anyone ever told you that Crocs are strictly for campsites or the garden only? You shouldn't be seen in public with them."

"I do wish I'd changed, but the Crocs stay."

"Suit yourself. The pub's only a few minutes away, and it's a nice day, so Charlie will most likely be outside."

We took a few side streets, then emerged on the edge of a row of shops with a pub beside an almost deserted car park. It was Monday afternoon, so understandably quiet, and many more rural pubs didn't even open at this time of day. We skirted around the back and emerged into a generous courtyard with picnic benches and a large marquee to accommodate smokers, where Charlie was greedily sipping a pint of something dark and thick.

"I guess that's him?" I whispered.

"How could you tell?" giggled Melody.

"The white uniform and the matching cap gives it away. I thought you said he went home for a sleep after he'd finished work?"

"He does, then he puts his uniform back on and comes out for his drinks. He usually eats here too. It's what he does."

"Why?"

"Because, like the rest of us, he gets hungry." Melody frowned.

"I meant, why put the uniform back on?"

"So everyone knows he's the milkman. Max, are you feeling okay?"

"Fine. It doesn't strike you as odd?"

"Of course it does! I was just messing with you. Let's go and have a word. If anyone knows anything, it's Charlie. If you think Sam's a gossip, wait until Charlie gets going. Be sure to buy him a drink. If you do that, he's guaranteed to talk."

Anxious was wary for some reason, and his hackles were up even though he didn't growl, but he remained by my side as we approached Charlie, the clearly eccentric milkman. He looked up as we got close, and smiled when he noted Melody.

"Well, look who it is! My favourite girl in the whole of Powys."

"I bet you say that to all the ladies," laughed Melody, seemingly good friends with Charlie.

"Only the pretty ones. Not like you to be boozing so early, Melody. I thought you were strictly a weekend drinker?"

"I'm showing Max here around, and it's not exactly a social visit. We wanted to have a chat with you, Charlie, if that's okay?"

Charlie's demeanour changed and he glanced down, then slowly lifted his head, his eyes welling. "A terrible business. Poor Del. He was a diamond, a true gent. He'll be sorely missed. How are you holding up? How's Bonnie and those sweet girls? They must be taking it really hard."

"They're coping, but it's been a rough day for everyone. Charlie, Max here was with me when we found Del this morning."

"I heard all about it."

"You did?" I asked. "Sorry, let me introduce myself properly. I'm Max, and this is Anxious."

"Aw, poor guy. What's the matter, little fella?" Charlie patted the bench and Anxious glanced at me, so I shrugged, leaving the choice to him, so after sniffing Charlie's leg and clearly thinking it was safe, he hopped up then accepted a head rub.

"It's his name, not his emotional state. A long story, and maybe for another time. Right now, we're trying to uncover information about Del's activities this morning."

"I know who killed him!" blurted Charlie, before draining his drink and holding it out.

"I'll get the beers in shall I?" I sighed, knowing this wouldn't be quick.

Chapter 10

Anxious was keen to come inside with me, so with a raised eyebrow to Melody, and her mouthing a silent, "Sorry," I nodded, took everyone's order, then hurried off. It was obvious Charlie was a major gossip, and revelled in whatever drama he could conjure up, so I wasn't exactly concerned by his "revelation." If he really did know who it was, he would have told the police, not waited for someone to buy him a pint so he could confess all.

The pub was quiet, just a lone customer and a bored looking woman behind the bar cleaning glasses. Her tight black curls and pale cheeks were in stark contrast to her shocking pink lipstick and matching vest, and when she saw me her eyes lit up immediately.

"Hello, stranger." She smiled warmly, eyes flashing dangerously, and I knew I was in for a hard time.

"Hi. Can I get a pint of Charlie's usual, and I'll have whatever medium cider is good and a pint of Guinness, too, please?"

"For you, darling, anything."

"Thanks."

"I'm Tina, and you are?"

"Max. Max Effort."

Tina glanced up from the pump while she held the glass at the perfect angle and the Guinness slowly rose, her eyebrows raised. "I bet you always give it max effort, eh, Max?" she giggled.

"I try my best."

"Sure you do, honey. Sure you do. So, what's a handsome hunk of a man doing in a place like this buying drinks for Charlie? Who's the Guinness for?"

"Melody. We've been hanging around together today."

"Oh!" Tina frowned, then brightened and asked, "Is it serious?"

"We're just friends. New friends."

"Tell me more?" Tina leaned forward, eyes intense, waiting for my answer.

"I'm afraid it's not anything like that. I was in the shop this morning, the deli, when Del was found. Have you heard?"

"Heard? Of course I have. Terrible business. Poor man. He was such a love. Real chatty type, not that he came in often. Not a drinker like Charlie out there, but he's harmless enough. He lives alone and isn't much of a cook, so we look after him here. Sorry that you had to find poor Del. Was it awful? What happened? We've heard some, but not all. Was he really in the alley, and stabbed?"

"I'm afraid so, yes. Have the police been in to question people?"

"Course they have. It's a murder, so they're all over everyone. Spoken to the local businesses already as far as I know. Two DIs came in early afternoon asking all kinds of questions. I told them Del was the best and nobody ever said a bad thing about him."

"Everyone liked him?"

"Everyone. Apart from that stuck up cow from the posh new shop around the corner."

I was intrigued, but tried not to show it. Finally, someone who might be worth talking to. "What does she sell?"

"That's just the thing. She's trying to take away poor Del's business. Not that it matters now, I suppose. She does the pastries, see. Sausage rolls, quiche, pork pies, all the pastry stuff. Poor Del was incensed, but he still did alright. He had his regulars and even if people do buy the odd sausage roll from her, he still does good. Did, I suppose, what with him being dead. A true sweetheart, was old Del. Proper old school, with nice manners. You don't get many like him now."

"So it was healthy competition?"

"You could call it that, or you could say she had no business coming here and stealing Del's customers. These newcomers ought to know better."

"When did she set up shop? Last year? This year?"

Tina leaned forward again, eyes dancing with mischief as she placed the last of the drinks on the bar, and hissed, "Ten years ago."

"Oh, right. Is there anything you can tell me about Del? Anything that might help figure this out?"

"You aren't the police. Why are you so interested?"

"Because I was there, and it was awful. I want to help. Melody is very upset, and I met his daughter and grandchildren earlier and they seemed so nice."

"Course. Sorry. But nothing comes to mind. Del was likeable and he'll be sorely missed. You find that killer, Max, and give him what for."

"I will."

After I paid, and got an earful from Anxious as I forgot to buy him any crisps or a fizzy drink, we headed back outside, but I paused at the door when Melody's high-pitched laugh rang out.

She and Charlie had their heads close and were talking quietly, but every so often one of them would laugh before checking nobody was close. For a distraught friend and long-time employee, she certainly seemed to have perked up a lot.

Anxious growled quietly, eyes locked on the pair, so I squatted beside him and asked, "Don't you trust Melody?"

He glanced at me before focusing on the others again, but was quiet, so I asked, "What about Charlie? Is he a good man?"

Anxious growled again, so I had my answer, at least as far as he was concerned. I wondered why my best buddy disliked him, but sometimes he didn't take to people, and I knew he wasn't a fan of those who drank too much. Or maybe it was the uniform, as there was that incident a few years ago when I'd taken him to a dairy supplier for a fancy restaurant I worked for, and he accidentally got trodden on by a man wearing a very similar outfit.

"Come on, let's get the drinks over to them and see what Charlie has to say."

As we approached, they both looked up and smiled, but it was obvious something wasn't quite right. "What's up?" I asked.

"Up? I'll tell you what's up. I was about to reveal the killer and you wandered off!" Charlie huffed, but nevertheless nodded his thanks when I set the drinks down.

"Thanks, Max." Melody took a sip and sighed. "Oh boy, that's good."

"I didn't mean to be rude, but I assumed you'd want a drink before you told us. Was that wrong?"

"No, just a bit off, Max." Charlie drained a third of his pint then set it down.

"You two been gossiping, have you?" I asked, my own cider very welcome. "Did you tell Melody who you think did it?"

"Not yet. And I don't gossip, I look out for folk around here. There's a difference. A big one. You be mindful of your manners around your elders, son."

"Of course. I was only pulling your leg. So, Charlie, care to share the information you have? Who do you think did it?"

"The newcomer. The posh one that runs the pastry shop. Sure, she's sweet enough and always pays her bill on time, but she's new and nobody trusts her. I know I wish I never had. Bad news, she is. She's all sweetness and light, but the truth comes out eventually."

"Charlie, she's been a part of this community for nigh on ten years. What on earth are you talking about? And she's not posh, she's from Newtown."

"Like I said, posh. Just because they have that fancy big supermarket, she thinks she's better than us. They get a bypass and reckon they're important. Who wants a bypass? It just means fewer people come to town."

"We have a Morrisons, and that big supermarket is nothing special. And besides, she doesn't shop there. She does a local shop like the rest of us."

"She's trouble, I tell you."

"What makes you say that?" I asked. "And what's her name?"

"Constance. See, proper posh. Even her name is all la di da." Charlie waved a hand around to emphasise his point, whatever that might have been.

"And why do you think she did it?"

"Max, you don't know people here like I do. I was around before most were even born and can remember them growing up and what their parents were like when young too. I'm an old man, but I know what I know. Constance is up herself, always has been. Her and Del didn't get on and that's nothing to do with Del but all to do with her. She was always trying to spread rumours about him, and trying to get people to stop going to the deli. It isn't right."

"What rumours? I never heard anything about that?" said Melody.

"You wouldn't, as nobody believed a word. She even told me that she heard Del was buying dodgy meat and that he lied about where it came from. People around here buy local, proper stuff, not European meat, or from New Zealand. What's the point of living in Wales where there are more sheep than people and then you go to the supermarket and buy lamb chops from New Zealand? It's nuts!" Charlie shook his head and had a drink. I couldn't argue with that, as he had a point.

"Del was fastidious about knowing the provenance of all his ingredients, you know that. I was telling Max earlier that he even travelled abroad to see suppliers to make sure it was top quality. Only if he couldn't source it locally, of course."

"That's right, and what I told Constance. Of course you have to buy Polish sausage from Poland. That makes sense. But no way did Del use dodgy meat for his own creations. You mark my words, she's trouble, that one."

"Then we better go and have a chat before she closes," I told Melody with a nod towards the car park.

"I think you're right. But before we go, I think Charlie better tell you what he told me."

"And what's that?"

Charlie focused on his pint and drained the glass, eyes downcast, then kept them like that once he'd set it down.

"What's wrong?" I asked.

Melody turned serious, which I wasn't expecting, as moments ago they'd both been laughing. "Tell him," she goaded.

"Don't wanna," mumbled Charlie, eyes roaming everywhere but to us.

"You have to. It's important."

"Fine. Del wasn't right. There was definitely something up. I don't like to speak ill of the dead, but he wasn't happy."

"I thought he loved his life? His job, his family, and you, Melody?"

"So did I. But Charlie thinks differently."

"What was the issue?"

"He couldn't get the quiche right," mumbled Charlie.

They burst out laughing, tears streaming, as Charlie added, "Del really hated a soggy bottom. Drove him nuts."

"It really did. It was the bane of his life. Normally, they were the best, but now and then something went wrong. Constance always gloated when it happened. Would tell everyone she had never in her life had a soggy bottom. He even mentioned it in his note."

I shook my head in warning, but it was too late.

Charlie's mirth died and his head snapped around as he asked, "What note?"

"Nothing. I shouldn't have said anything. It isn't important."

"Don't give me that, girl. What note?"

"I'm not a girl. I'm a woman approaching forty and you need to stop calling women girls. It's rude."

"It's just my way. I didn't mean anything by it. And you've never mentioned it before. Stop trying to change the subject."

"I'm not. We have to go. We need to speak with Constance." Melody rose, drained her pint, and wiped her lips, then I stood too.

Charlie grabbed my arm, stopping me from leaving, and asked, "Is there something I should know? What's this about a note?"

"We can't tell you. Sorry, but the police said not to. It's nothing for you to worry about."

"Of course it is, otherwise you'd tell me. We have a killer on the loose in our community. Everyone's scared, and sad that Del's gone. I demand to be told!"

"Charlie, you let Max go right this instant. It's my fault, as I shouldn't have said anything, but Max is right. It's not your concern."

"Oh, but it is yours? A stranger, and Del's employee? How convenient," he sneered.

"What's that supposed to mean?" snapped Melody, batting Charlie's hand so he released me.

"You know what it means. You two are up to something. How do I know it wasn't you two that killed him?"

"Because you know me, and if I say Max is a good guy that should be enough for you. Don't you trust my word?"

"Yes, of course I do. Sorry. I'm just down in the dumps. You go do your investigating, I'm after another pint or three." Charlie shoved to his feet and hobbled off without another word.

"Max, I'm so sorry. It's the stress. Charlie's a good man, and he was close to Del, so don't be too harsh on him."

"I understand. Let's get going. We need to speak to this Constance."

Anxious hurried ahead, but paused when we reached the car park. He knew better than to run anywhere where there could be traffic, so walked to heel rather than be put on the lead. It had crept up on me slowly, but I now realised that he hardly ever went on the lead as he had now got so much experience in so many different places and understood when it was time to go and play and when he had to be cautious.

After we crossed the car park and were on the pavement, Melody pulled me to a stop. "I'm sorry I mentioned the note. My mouth runs away with me sometimes."

"Don't worry about it. This is a difficult time, and we're trying our best. These things happen."

"But you seem so cool. Aren't you stressed? Worried? Max, your name was on that letter. Does the killer know about you? What if they read it?"

"I've considered all of that, and I don't think they did. Del left it for us to find, and that's what happened. And I may seem confident and relaxed, but this does have me stressed, I assure you. Maybe it's because I've been around things like this before, and of course it's not my loved one that is dead. It's much harder for you. What I would like to know is why you and Charlie were looking so happy earlier. When I went to get the drinks. You looked suspicious. Is he a concern?"

"I was trying to get information from him, so was laughing at one of his lame jokes. Max, relax, it's all good.

Maybe not good, but you can trust Charlie. He's been around for like ever, same as Sam in the shop. They're his buddies."

"I'll take your word for it. What did Charlie actually say about Del? What did they talk about this morning?"

"Nothing of interest. Only the usual banter. He told you Del seemed distracted lately, didn't he?"

"I was there for that, sure."

"There isn't much to say. He said Del seemed a little off lately, talked about the quiche a lot. I know we made a big joke about it, but he hated that he got teased over it. It makes me wonder why he mentioned it in the note. That was odd, right?"

"I assumed he was just being funny. That it was an in joke."

"It is, so it's probably nothing, but the fact he mentioned it to the milkman is peculiar."

"You don't think there could be more to it, do you?"

"Like what?"

"I have absolutely no clue. He wasn't poisoned. At least I don't think he was. I wonder if…"

"Max, you're scaring me. What are you thinking?"

"Could Del have been poisoned first, then stabbed? Maybe he knew his time was almost up, so wrote the note, then he collapsed and the killer finished him off."

"Then we better get back to the community centre before anyone eats the quiche!"

In a panic, we dashed back to Vee—she started first time with a happy belch—then raced through the one-way system while Melody tried, and failed, to get an answer from Veronica.

"She must have forgotten about her phone. She said it was still in her car." Melody ended the call and glanced at me in a panic.

"Don't worry, we'll be there soon. What time does she open the food bank?"

Melody checked her watch and groaned. "Five minutes ago."

"It'll be fine. Did we even pack the quiche?"

"You tell me. You're the one who loaded up the boxes."

"Then yes, we packed the quiche. Soggy bottom or not, they looked lovely, and to be honest I totally forgot about them not being perfect. Everything looked so good, and nothing should be wasted anyway."

"That's true, but not if it means we've murdered dozens of people because we gave them dodgy quiche."

I willed Vee to go faster, but when we hit a set of traffic lights for non-existent roadworks, I truly began to panic. Several unbearable minutes later, we were on our way again, and made it to the food bank soon enough, but by the time I skidded to a stop, okay, juddered, our nerves were frayed and we had both imagined the worst. The fact there weren't scores of dead bodies littering the car park of the small community centre was a good start, and when we saw Veronica and she waved, we both sighed with relief.

Then we saw the remains of the quiches on the table, hardly anything left, and as I glanced around I groaned when I saw scores of people eating them and other fresh offerings from Del's Deli.

"We need a plan," I told Melody.

"No, what we need is an alibi. And a good one. We're in big trouble if we kill all the needy people."

"Then we better check everyone's alright and try to stop any more poisoned quiche being given away."

We hurried over to the long tables where people were being given bags of groceries or sampling Del's quality wares, calling for Veronica to stop what she was doing and to start packing instead.

Chapter 11

"What's all this racket?" asked Veronica with a frown as she handed over a bag for life to a woman with two excited children already delving into the groceries while they popped the last of their quiche into their eager mouths.

"We need a word. It's urgent," gasped Melody, watching in horror as the children were given another slice.

"There might be an issue with the quiche," I whispered, glancing at the woman and children and shaking my head.

Veronica nodded, then told the children, "Sorry, but the quiche is off," and grabbed for it. It was no use, and the young ones stepped away and hurriedly gobbled the cheesy treat. I had to admit, it looked lovely, and with no soggy bottom that I could see.

Distracted, their mother didn't even notice, and wandered off, the children chasing ahead after poking their tongues out at me.

"Is there much left?" I asked.

"What's going on?" Veronica had a word with the woman helping her, then came from behind the table and took us to one side. "Is there a problem?"

"We got in a panic and wondered if maybe Del had been poisoned first. Maybe someone nobbled the quiche and that was why he... Um, never mind about the details, but we need to check everyone's alright. Has anyone felt poorly?"

"Anyone collapse or have a funny turn?" asked Melody, eyes roaming like mine, trying to check on everyone at once.

"You two need to calm down. Everything is fine. Nearly all the fresh food has gone. Much of it eaten here. The number of people we've had already means nobody got that much, but they said it was lovely. And besides, haven't you tried it yourselves? I know you kept a little something back to give Del a proper send off in the way he'd have wanted."

Melody and I exchanged a guilty look, and I admitted, "We have, and it was the best. Del was a true artisan. I, er, I think we might have got carried away and thought the worst. We were trying to figure this out, and when we thought about the fresh food, we suspected maybe he'd been poisoned before he was stabbed. I guess we were wrong."

"If he was poisoned, it could have been anything. A sausage roll, the quiche, even some olives. Maybe it was just one quiche, but they've gone now, as you can see." We turned to see the last slice being eaten by an elderly gentleman, then he chatted with the woman before taking his bag of groceries and hobbling off, smiling.

"Then either we're too late, or nothing is wrong with the food." Melody grimaced, then crossed her arms and glared at me.

"Hey, why are you giving me the daggers? We both thought the same thing."

"Only because you put the idea in my head. This was dumb. Veronica, we're so sorry to come barging back here and stressing you out."

"It's not a problem, but it sure is a relief." She wiped her forehead with her sleeve and smiled at us. "Everyone relies on us, and this is important, so we have to be so careful about what we give people. It's why it's usually tinned goods rather than fresh. That way, we know it's fine. But who could pass on Del's amazing grub? Everyone loved him around here, not that most people here ever got to have much as they can't afford it, but today has been a real treat for them. At least something good came from his death. Not that I'm saying I'm glad he's gone," she added hurriedly.

"Of course not. We're so sorry. Can we hang around for a while to ensure nothing happens?" I asked.

"If you're going to do that, then make yourselves useful. You can sort out a few bags for people."

Although time was getting on we decided to stay for a while to be sure everyone was safe, so helped pack the bags for people, asking them what they wanted, sure to give them a varied selection. I was shocked by the numbers that passed from one end of the table to the other, and the mix of people that were in need of assistance to help make ends meet.

After ten minutes it was clear there were no casualties from Del's quiche, so we apologised for having to leave, but we really needed to visit Constance in the pastry shop before she closed, so once again piled into Vee and headed back to the high street to have a word.

Neither of us said much on the short drive, happy to focus on the fact we weren't responsible for poisoning those in need, so when we pulled up and got out, it was with a loud sigh that made us both smile before we walked along the row of shops then paused outside All Things Pastry.

"Wow, she likes to do a fancy display," I noted, admiring the artistry of the shop window.

"Constance is a real stickler for presentation. Del even took a few tips from how she does things, not that he would ever admit it. He really upped his game once she opened up, and always ensured his displays were as good as hers. Different styles, but they both really care about food, and if I'm being honest, Constance is an excellent cook and never skimps on her pie fillings. Del wasn't so into the pies, so that worked out perfectly and people come to both shops for different things. There's no fresh meats here, or much of what we offer, so the competition isn't as bad as people like Charlie make out. He's just a grumpy man who doesn't like change."

"Even though she's been here for over ten years? That's not exactly new to the area, is it?"

"No, but that's his way. He's harmless enough and loves the town, but he's been here a long time and seen a lot of change. Not all of it for the good. Constance can be hard work though. She's not always the easiest to get along with, so be patient if you want her to talk. And once she gets going, she won't stop. She's a right chatterbox if she likes you."

"Then we better make a good impression." I went to open the door, but Melody took my arm and stopped me. "Problem?"

"You can't take Anxious inside. I know he goes everywhere with you, but dogs aren't allowed. It's a hygiene thing."

"Of course. I understand. And sorry for bringing him into the deli. I should have known better."

"Max, Del allowed dogs inside, so don't worry about that. But lots of shops won't let you, and Constance is a stickler for the rules."

I explained to the little guy, who wasn't happy about missing out on the remaining tasty delights he could see through the window, but he made do with a biscuit once I'd clipped him to a railing.

The interior was as I'd expected it to be. It smelled fresh, the mix of various pastry based offerings a sheer delight to the senses, but it went beyond that. Whereas Del's was all about tradition and endless wooden shelving, Constance's was light and airy with bleached wood giving a washed out, summer vibe, with rather more ribbons, bows, and bunting than I'd have liked, but it certainly screamed quality, and was pricey too.

Her food was laid out expertly, but it was the end of the day and most of the fresh stuff had been sold. I wondered if she'd done better than usual because of Del's demise, and by the smile on her face as she served what would be one of her last customers of the day, I guessed I was right.

We nodded to the woman as she left, and approached the counter where Constance was re-arranging the few remaining pies and several delicious looking sausage rolls with perfectly golden pastry.

She glanced up and asked, "Hi, what will it be?" then her smile faded as she noted Melody. "Oh, Melody, I'm so sorry to hear the news. It's just awful. You poor thing." She hurried around the glass display that served as a counter and wrapped her thin arms around a rather shocked Melody.

On full alert, as who stood to gain more than her, I watched as a flicker of a smug smile crossed Constance's face before she held Melody at arm's length and shook her head sadly.

"Um, thanks." Melody stepped back a pace, clearly uncomfortable with the sudden display of affection. "It was a terrible shock and nobody knows quite what to do. Have you spoken to the police?"

Constance was average height, but her slight build made her seem to loom over Melody, her fuller figure giving the impression she was shorter than she was. Constance's wild head of brown curly hair gave her a good few inches extra and her heels certainly helped. Rather heavily made-up, her face was line-free and glowing, partly from the heat of the shop, but also because she wore a thick cashmere jumper of bright orange over a pair of simple black trousers. When she shook her head, her curls bounced. I wondered how many birds you could get to nest in there. Quite a few, by my estimation.

"You poor thing." Constance ignored the question and reached out her hands in sympathy, but Melody rubbed at her face and smoothed down her top. "What a blow to the community."

"It really is. Bonnie and the girls are understandably distraught, and she had to go to the station. So did we."

"We?" Constance's eyes drifted to me and I smiled in greeting.

"This is Max. He was there when Del was found. We both were. What did the police say?"

"Delighted, I'm sure." Constance offered a rather limp hand, so I shook it.

"Hi. Nice to meet you."

"And you, Max. Why are you involved in this?" she asked, eyes narrowing. "Did the police give him the all clear?" she asked Melody. "What's your role in this, Max?"

"Max is a freelance investigator," said Melody, nudging me to play along.

"Strictly private. I just happened to be in the right place at the right time."

"How intriguing. And to answer your question, Melody, yes I have spoken to the police just like everyone else has. Two detectives came and took my statement and we had quite a long chat about how well I knew Del and what kind of relationship we had. You know how it was with us. Rivals, but all in good spirits. Unlike some others around here, I don't try to badmouth the competition."

"Del never said a bad word about you to anyone!" Melody stepped forward then clearly thought better of it and shifted back beside me like she needed the backup.

"Of course not, and regardless of what that gossip Charlie says, I never told people Del couldn't make quality quiche. He was an artist, like me, and we both take, or in his case, took, pride in our work."

"Charlie just likes to cause trouble. He's innocent enough. But you do tell customers your sausage rolls are better."

"That's just good business." Constance waved it away as unimportant, but there was a hint of amusement, like she knew something we didn't. "It's been terribly busy today, but I took no pleasure in it. It's only because Del's is shut. What will happen now? Will the shop remain closed? I suppose it will without him." The light tone was less than subtle, even though she was trying to hide her excitement about being the main shop in town now.

"For now, it is shut, yes. It depends what happens with the will and what Bonnie decides to do. But that's not why we're here. We want to talk to you about Del."

"Then ask away, although I can't imagine what I can tell you. We weren't exactly close friends, and our relationship was never the best even though I tried my hardest to make it work. Ten years, Melody, and some still treat me like an outsider. I'm only from Newtown! What is wrong with people?"

"That wasn't how Del was, or how I am. You belong here the same as the rest of us, but you have to admit that you've got plenty to gain from Del being gone."

Constance bristled and snapped, "Don't you dare accuse me! I have every right to run my shop and, yes, of course my business will increase, but I would never hurt him or anyone. Ask the detectives. I told them everything that happened this morning."

"What did happen? Something different than usual?" I asked.

"Why, yes, as a matter of fact it did. It started off in the usual way. Every morning, once Del and I had finished our bakes, one or the other of us would go and look through the window of our rival to see what we were up against for the day. The usual competitive nature of the business, I'm afraid. This morning started like that. He was around here about seven nosing at the glass, but rather than just wave then leave, he knocked, so I let him in as I was finishing arranging my pies."

"That's not like him," said Melody.

"No, that's what I thought. He seemed rather tired, although aren't we always with the hours we keep? Anyway, I let him in and he never said a word, just stood in the middle of the shop and stared at the pies."

"Then what happened?"

"He asked if I ever thought about leaving. About shutting down and going away. I laughed, thinking he was joking, as everyone knew he loved the deli more than anything. It was a shock. I told him I never wanted to leave, that I was happy, and I asked if he was. He was distracted, and kept mumbling, then mentioned something about going off in a van. I think he'd been up late watching TV or something and wasn't properly awake, although he'd been up for hours, obviously."

"Then what happened?" prompted Melody when Constance's attention drifted to the door as someone walked past.

"Eh? Sorry, this has shaken me up, I don't mind admitting. Nothing much. He stayed a while longer, then left without saying another word. It was odd, out of character, and I wasn't sure why he'd even come inside."

"That's not like him. He didn't seem scared?"

"Del? I've never seen the man scared in his life. Apart from when he tried to compare his quiche to mine. Poor man hated that my beauties were always better."

"And didn't you like to tell everyone!" growled Melody, bristling like Anxious when faced with a rabbit that didn't realise it was meant to run away.

"I tell it like it is. Now, are we done? I'm sorry this has happened, and I truly mean that, but I do have to shut up now. It's been a very long day, and I'm sure even longer and much more stressful for you. Maybe you should go home and rest?"

"I can't rest until I know Del's killer will be found. I'm watching you, Constance. You can count on it." Melody pointed to her own eyes then jabbed two fingers out in warning.

"There's no need for that! We can be friends. I always wanted to be, but you never gave me the chance. Maybe you could come and work for me? I will probably need the extra help now we'll be so busy." Constance smiled sweetly, but there was an obvious tone, and for a moment I thought Melody was going to lunge.

To her credit, she composed herself, smiled, then said, "Thank you for the offer, but I'll pass. It hasn't even been a day yet, so maybe you're speaking out of turn."

"If I caused offence, I apologise."

Both women eyed the other for long enough to make it uncomfortable, so I took Melody's arm and gently led her to the door. Before we left, Melody turned back into the shop and asked, "Did Del mention anything else? Even the slightest thing?"

"Yes, what about why he was acting so strange?"

"We didn't have that kind of relationship. Like I said, it was most peculiar and he was most likely tired but wanted to see what I was selling today."

We left Constance to pack away the remains of the day; I heard her whistling as the door closed.

Anxious was fretting, worried we'd eaten all the pies without him, but he perked up once we walked along the high street a little, the memory fading along with the smells. Once far enough away from the shop, I asked Melody if she was alright and she burst into tears.

"Let's go back to mine and I'll cook you a nice dinner. How does that sound?"

"Max, you've done more than enough, and I don't want to put you to any trouble."

"It's no trouble, and everyone has to eat. I'd be cooking anyway, and I think we'd both like some company today. Maybe you shouldn't be alone. Come on, it'll do you good. I promise it won't be too late, but we should go now if you are coming."

"Then yes, I'd love to. I'll meet you there so you don't have to drive me back into town later."

We agreed that Melody would come in an hour, so she had time to freshen up and get changed. Anxious and I headed off, a little quiet time welcome so I could think things through and put the day into some kind of order after meeting so many new faces.

Chapter 12

I was in my element back at the airfield. The kitchen was arranged and good to go, so while Anxious crawled under Vee for some much-needed rest after a busy day, I set about making a simple but generously portioned one-pot wonder of chicken stew with a loaf of bread from the bakery I'd picked up earlier.

No sooner had it begun to simmer away and my work was done for at least an hour, and I'd eased into my chair, the detectives, Laura and Bishop, arrived unexpectedly. They wore the same clothes as that morning, Laura in a simple black faded suit with white blouse, Bishop in his supermarket clobber and scuffed shoes, his deep tan the only thing that made him look at least a little healthy and happy.

"Wish we could take it easy," sighed Bishop, glancing at the bubbling pot. "Smells nice."

"Thanks. It's just a chicken stew. Melody is coming over for dinner. She's had a rough day and I thought it would be best if she had company."

"That's very kind of you. Mind if we sit?" asked Laura.

"Sure. Let me get the other chair." I grabbed the third one from the rear of the van and set it out so they could both sit, then I offered them a drink, which they declined.

"I was hoping you'd call and say you'd solved the case," said Laura, smiling, her blue eyes with the dark make-up sparkling with amusement.

"No such luck. I've been trying, but the only person who had even the slightest bad thing to say about Del was Constance, and even she seemed to like him really, or at least appreciate his work and business acumen."

"We got the same impression. Did she tell you about Del acting strange this morning?"

"She did. As far as I can tell, he got into watching travel stuff online as the twins are into it at the moment. Bonnie said they go through phases faster than hot dinners, but this one seems to have stuck around more than usual. They already knew about me, apparently."

"Yes, quite a few people do. The twins, and Bonnie, seem lovely, and we hated to have to question Del's daughter, but she was helpful."

"Do you have any leads? For a while I thought maybe Del had been poisoned."

"What gave you that idea?" asked Bishop, leaning forward, eyes glued to me.

"I'm not sure. The fact the death is so odd. That he had time to write me a message. It makes no sense."

"It doesn't," admitted Laura. "It sure has us stumped. So we have no leads, just idle gossip from the old-timers and people saying it might have been Constance because she's new to these parts."

"Only been here for ten years. That's practically yesterday for some of them." Bishop was dripping sarcasm and clearly had a run-in with Charlie and suffered him complaining about the out-of-towners.

"But you don't think it was Constance?"

"She isn't the type. She's competitive, and is pleased she can clean up now Del's is closed, but murder? Very unlikely. The only way that woman would ever get her hands dirty is with flour and pie filling."

"Anything on his computer? Are you allowed to say?"

"Nothing of note. Just business stuff, online history of checking you out and watching way too many videos about vans and comparing models, but that's about it." Bishop shrugged, then added, "What does surprise us is that a man like Del, a workaholic and real family guy, seemed genuinely interested in packing it all in and going travelling. He doesn't sound the type."

"I wasn't until I realised life was too short to always be working and chasing money when the important stuff was getting neglected. Now I can't believe I left it so long."

"Del was different, and much older. Almost retirement age, although guys like him never really retire. Max, the reason we stopped by, apart from to see if you had any information, is to ask you a very important question."

"Okay?" I said warily, not liking how serious they'd become.

"Why are you here? I mean, why stick around? You do realise it makes you seem very suspicious, don't you?"

"Does it? Why?"

"Because Del directed a letter to you, and here you are, pally with his assistant, spending time with his daughter and grandchildren. Shouldn't you be keeping a low profile?"

"I think I'm doing the right thing. I'm involved whether I like it or not, so I want to get to the bottom of this. You said that was alright and I could talk to people and see what I could uncover. Have you changed your minds?"

"It's not that we've changed our minds, it's that we genuinely can't figure you out, Max. You're a real dark horse. On the one hand, you're like a knight in shining armour come to save the residents of small towns from the bad guys and get justice."

"Like a sheriff in the Wild West," laughed Laura.

"Yes, or the Lone Ranger. But on the other hand, you seem to get involved in way too many things like this. You have to understand how suspicious that makes you from our point of view. Maybe you planted the note as you wanted some action after taking it easy for a few months." Bishop held up his hand to stop me speaking and said, "Yeah, yeah, we know it wasn't your handwriting, and we know it was Del's, but it's so downright weird. I guess what I'm saying is this has us scratching our heads."

"So I'm not a suspect?"

"Not really." Laura placed her hands in her lap, perfectly composed, and asked, "Are you holding out on us? We wouldn't like it if you are. We're sharing what we know so far, which is not a lot, so hope you're doing likewise."

"I am, but there's not much to say beyond what's obvious."

"And that is?" asked Laura.

"That what Del wrote is the truth. Which means he believed he was about to die. And that somehow he knew I was in the area. I'm guessing that's just information someone must have posted on a forum or something. You didn't find anything like that?"

"Not yet, but it seems like he and the twins were members of some of those sites where the posts vanish after a minute or two, and we don't have the kind of clout to get that data retrieved, not that we even know if anything's there. So, cards on the table time? We have nothing but a bunch of local gossip and no leads so far."

"And all I have is that I'm convinced Del knew I was heading into town somehow and wrote me the note as for whatever reason he knew he was about to die."

"Then for now, we're done, but keep in touch, Max, and don't hold out on us." Laura stood, and stared down at me, serious and silent, then she winked, smiled, and nodded to Bishop.

Her partner sighed, then heaved from the chair and rubbed his back. "Don't know how you can sit in these things."

"You get used to it," I laughed, then stood to shake hands before they left in their smart white Subaru.

As they drove off, Melody arrived in her old Mitsubishi, so I explained what had happened then we decided to have a glass of wine before dinner and settled to discuss the events of the day. Her first question surprised me.

"Do you think he did it to himself?"

"Suicide, you mean?"

"I guess." Melody hid behind her wine, but her deep sadness was evident. "Everyone is saying he wasn't himself this morning, that he was talking about leaving. I know he was going along with the girls and their travel fancies, but what if it made him realise he'd been doing the wrong thing all these years and he should have been off having adventures like you? Or those people in the videos they were watching?"

"Melody, you said it yourself that Del did whatever it took to hold on to the property and his business, even with all the trouble his ex-wife caused, and then raised Bonnie there. It was his life. Sure, I expect there were times when he wished things were different, but doesn't everyone?"

"Of course."

"Then he was just like the rest of us. But you knew him better than anyone except Bonnie, so what do you think? Be honest. You can tell me anything, and don't forget that I didn't know Del. Don't feel bad if you have something negative to say. I can tell how much he meant to you."

"Del truly was a wonderful man. Yes, we had our moments, as he was utterly obsessed with getting everything just right, and the hours in the shop drove me nuts, but he seemed happy. He always had a kind word to say about everyone, would help whenever he could, and was an important part of the community. He never had a real argument with anyone, not even Constance, regardless of how she spins it."

"So he never spoke of leaving?"

"Never. He adored it, and he adored his town. As I told you, even when he went on holiday it was usually to see suppliers in Europe. He enjoyed that a lot, and bored me to tears with the details when he came home, but leave? Give it up? No. And he wasn't depressed, and certainly not suicidal, so no way did he stab himself in the throat after writing you a note."

"So it's settled. A man who did nobody any harm, and spent most of his time in the shop with you, and if not then it was with Bonnie and the twins. They're really close, aren't they?"

"Very. I'm kind of envious, or was, as although I'm close to my sister, and I told you she's into camping and travelling, it's not like their relationship was. After Del split from his wife it was him and Bonnie. He worked like a madman to ensure she was brought up right and had what she needed, but that meant Bonnie worked in the shop too. She left when she could, which is fair enough, but he never complained about it. He just got on with things. Same as he always did."

"I wish I could have met him. He sounds like a great guy."

"He would have loved you. You two would have got on like a house on fire. Talking about food and swapping recipes, and he'd probably pick your brains about vanlife so he could tell the girls and sound like he knew what he was talking about."

"We would have talked for hours, I'm sure, but sadly that's not to be. Now, how about we have a meal in his honour? Dinner is almost ready. Let's get things sorted. I know this is a terrible day for you, and I hope I'm not overstepping by asking you to spend a few hours with me."

"Of course not. Max, it's exactly what I needed. Better than sitting at home alone. I don't have any close friends, so this is exactly what I need. Someone to talk to."

"What about your sister?"

"She knows what happened and offered to come over, but I said no. Sometimes she can be a bit much, and I'm not in the mood for her today. I feel better for talking to you. What can I do to help? Shall I set out the bowls? Are we eating here?"

"Unless you want to sit inside Vee?"

"Here's great. I like this place. It's so peaceful, and when it's dark, the lights from everyone's pitches look incredible."

We set everything up like we were an old married couple, falling into an easy routine of passing things around and arranging the small coffee table. Anxious made an appearance, clearly wiped out by the day as normally when we had guests he'd be all over them instantly, so I gave him his dinner then Melody and I settled and ate ours, her compliments welcome.

After I insisted on washing up afterwards while she relaxed, I joined her for a glass of wine, hers a small one as she was driving, and as night fell and the lights came on around the site, she was right and it did look beautiful. I lit a small fire, and we scooted out from under the gazebo and got so close that our knees were toasty, enjoying the crackle and the shimmering lights that made the airfield feel like a truly magical place.

"Hey, what's that?" Anxious and Melody turned as I pointed across the airfield where lights flickered, but I was sure they were in a line. "It's not a real runway, is it?"

"That is the original runway, yes. Nowadays, they use it for something entirely different."

"Like what?" I stood and moved away from the fire, shielding my eyes to see better, but it remained a series of faint, shimmering lights like they were many miles away.

"Why don't we go and see? I think you'll enjoy it. It doesn't happen every night, sometimes not for months, so you're in for a real treat. Normally, these things get posted online and everyone comes, but I hadn't even thought to check. I should have, because of course they'd do it tonight."

"Melody, I have no idea what you're talking about, but I am intrigued. Let me get Anxious' lead as it's dark and I don't want to lose him, then can we take a look?"

"Of course we can. It's just what we need. I wonder if Bonnie and the girls will come too."

"Why would they?"

"Just wait and see."

Anxious was as excited as always by the prospect of a walk, and I was beyond intrigued by the mystery, not that I needed any more in my life right now, but my curiosity had got the better of me. Melody led the way across the site, both of us with head torches on the lowest setting as they were beyond annoying if someone was talking to you and the light shone right in your face. Luckily, I'd invested in quality rechargeable ones that you could angle down to the ground, so we could talk without blinding each other. When we got closer, we turned them off, and Melody stopped us at the edge of the old runway where the ground was harder underfoot and the grass very stunted.

We stood side by side, with Anxious sitting, his head cocked, glancing at me occasionally. I shrugged, as in the dark as him, noting others coming from across the site and lining the edge of the runway. It already felt otherworldly with everyone's torches, like a working airfield, but this was not for planes, it was for vehicles and people.

A convoy stretched out, approaching us slowly. As it passed those ahead of us, they joined the line, it getting longer and longer as it closed in, the lights truly magical.

"What's happening?"

Melody turned and smiled. "It's everyone's way of paying their respects to the dead. Sometimes it's a local, other times it's a vanlifer, or a relative they ask others to celebrate their life by doing the procession. It's been going on for years, but has got more popular recently. The last couple of years it's become a real local tradition. Look, there's Bonnie and the twins." Melody waved, then grabbed me and dashed forward. Anxious trotted beside me and we joined everyone walking in a line, then caught up with Bonnie and the twins.

"Hi, everyone," I said, not sure what to say.

"Uncle Max, you came!" cheered one of the twins, before the smile faded and she moved closer to her mum and sister.

"I didn't know this was a thing, but I'm glad I'm here."

"Grampy would have wanted it, especially since he was so into vans and travelling like us now," said the other girl.

"He would love it," agreed her sister.

"He'd be very touched," agreed Bonnie, noting my presence with a heavy smile and a faint nod. "Dad enjoyed this place on occasion, but what he mostly liked were the people. The girls have been begging me to come for weeks and we've made a few trips to chat to people as they seem obsessed with anything van related, so this would mean so much to Del."

"And this happens for everyone who passes?" I asked, trying to be as diplomatic as possible.

"Not everyone, but a lot of people. We've been several times before. The girls enjoy the lights and the party mood, but we don't stay late." Bonnie moved closer and whispered, "It gets quite wild."

For the next several minutes, we walked in silence, people in front joining the back of the line until we reached the end of the runway. Then we made a single circuit of the entire airfield, the procession so long you could look across and see the lights of those behind and in front, until it became a continues line with no front or end, before we suddenly stopped, a loud cheer went out, and then the procession broke apart and the site erupted with noise.

Bonnie and the girls left before it got wild, and as the night wore on I understood why. This was a true wake in the old tradition, everyone drinking, dancing, shouting, and partying to music that blared from various vans across the site.

Nobody would be getting much sleep, Anxious and I included, so we did what everyone else did, and with Melody deciding to stay the night now the party had begun, we drank, laughed, and celebrated the life of a great man I wished I could have met, but had only encountered once he'd left for the big kitchen in the sky.

Chapter 13

The morning came all too soon, but I rose at seven regardless of the lack of sleep, and was surprised by how fresh I felt. The evening festivities had been a whirlwind of chaos, and I took a while to warm to things but eventually got into the swing of it, and let my hair down and became immersed in the party vibe.

Different people and communities treated death in very different ways, but here close to the Wales/England border they had their own, very unorthodox way of celebrating a person's life. I liked it.

Sure, there were tears, and plenty of grief from those who knew and loved Del, but many only knew him in passing yet wanted to give him a proper send off regardless. For many airfield residents it was nothing but an excuse to party, but they understood the importance for the locals and acted accordingly.

Melody stirred from the pop-top bed, little more than an awkward crawl space with a platform; I didn't envy her the cramped conditions, having used it myself several times when Min visited before we decided we'd be fine on the bed. I had offered to let Melody take the better bed, but she would hear none of it and crawled into the cubby gratefully at whatever the ridiculous hour was we'd finally got home.

I opened up, put coffee on to brew, a proper pot for the morning rather than instant, then went and used the long drop composting toilets I both loathed and adored as without some sort of facilities my vanlife would be very different and much more inconvenient. Time for a portable toilet maybe? The issue was, VW vans like mine were not exactly spacious, so I had absolutely nowhere to put it. I had considered one of those ingenious collapsible versions, but doing my business into what was basically a bucket with a bag in appealed even less than the alternative.

After a wash, I returned and brushed my teeth at the van, sorted through some clothes, then hurriedly changed before Melody got up. With Anxious skipping about, revitalised by his sleep and excited about having a guest stay over, I poured the coffee, sure the fresh aromas would rouse Melody. While I waited, I sipped happily as I did a few circuits around the van to get the blood flowing and see what was happening at my temporary home.

All was quiet bar a few fellow early risers, but I was shocked to see Bonnie and the twins pull up then exit the car. Anxious raced over, barking, but the girls made him be quiet and I could hear them warning him about other people still sleeping. They really were sweet kids, and clearly well-behaved, so Bonnie left them to play a quiet game of hide and seek while she wandered over, eyes scouring the site as if searching for something. What could that be? A pang of guilt hit as I wondered if I'd been lax in not suspecting her of this awful crime, as she seemingly had plenty to gain by inheriting the business, but what little I knew of her, and her entire demeanour, made me certain she was not the killer.

If not her, then who? Constance was clearly secretly pleased to have the extra business, and most likely keeping her fingers crossed that Bonnie would never open the shop again, but what about the other characters I'd met? Killer milkman? Vengeful newsagent owner? Barmaid with a secret she wished to keep and would go to any lengths to ensure remained hidden? Or someone even closer? I glanced back at Vee as Melody made an appearance and again felt a rush of guilt as my thoughts turned dark.

There had to be something else, a way to explain everything that made sense, but so far it eluded me. And yet, there at the back of my mind, lurking like a sneak in the night, was the truth of this. I sensed the knowledge slowly rising to the surface like a bubble from the deep released by those weird frightening fish that never see the light of day, but I knew that this snippet of information would present itself soon enough. I just needed a trigger to let it pop on the cusp of my awareness and I'd have the answer everyone craved.

So for now, I'd simply let things simmer, continue doing what I had been doing, and I knew the answer would come. It was inspiring, as ever since this had begun I felt this was one mystery that might never be solved as it was beyond inexplicable. But this morning, in the fresh light of day, I knew that wasn't true. Of course it wasn't! Del had written that note to me, so of course it had happened, as impossible as it seemed. All that remained was to understand the timeline and figure out the conundrum.

I waved as Bonnie approached after pausing to look over the airfield and check on her children. Seemingly satisfied, she picked up her pace and arrived with a tired but friendly smile.

"Good morning," I said.

"Morning. I wasn't sure if you'd be up yet. The girls have been driving me mad since just after five, saying we should have stayed last night. I didn't think it was the right place for young children, but maybe they're right. I promised we could come early so they could see you. Is that alright?"

"Was it me they wanted to see, or Anxious?" I laughed. "And of course it's fine. Bonnie, it was a great party, and a send-off you can be proud of, but you're right, and it wasn't the best place for young children still grieving."

"It was so kind of everyone to pay their respects, and I spoke to a lot of people on the way back to the car last night, but I was too overwhelmed. Does that make sense?"

"Absolutely! It was a shock for you all, and so much happened yesterday. Don't concern yourself with it. Melody stayed over in the pop-top bed but I think I heard her getting up, so she should be out soon."

"So she spent the night?"

"Um, yes, but just as a friend, of course."

"Absolutely!" Bonnie checked the van, then pulled me away and we walked for a while before she asked, "Did she say anything? Mention Dad and what happened?"

"How'd you mean? Is there a problem?"

"I'm not sure. Max, I didn't sleep a wink last night. Everything kept going around and around in my head until I felt like I was going mad. Dad's gone, and forever, and it's left a massive hole in my life. The girls too. They adored him. Everything's gone wrong and I don't know if I'm coming or going."

"I'm so sorry, but that's a natural reaction to a terrible thing. Maybe take it easy today and go back to bed. The girls won't be going to school, I assume?"

"Not this week, no. They loved him so much and keep saying it's their fault because they got Del excited about travelling with them. That they bet if he wasn't so tired from staying up late he would never have been killed."

"The poor things. But that's not why you came, is it? What's this about Melody?"

"I'm sure it's nothing, and I do think very highly of her, but I can't shake the feeling she knows something. Gosh, here I am telling a complete stranger who was also there when my father was found murdered that I'm concerned about the woman who did more than anyone, even me, for Dad. I'm so stupid. Forgive me. I don't even know what I'm saying."

"Bonnie, you can tell me. It's your choice, of course, but if it's important then just say it."

"That's just it, I don't even know what's important and what isn't. You are on the level, aren't you?" Bonnie was a mess of nervous tics, chewing at her lip, her right eye twitching, wringing her hands then smoothing down her shirt, while her foot tapped and she checked on the girls then Vee constantly as if waiting for something terrible to happen and for the rest of her world to come crashing down around her.

I did the only thing I could think of and wrapped her in my arms. She trembled, but I held her tight, and gradually she relaxed until she was almost limp. I took her weight easily and let her cry it out. When the tears had subsided as they inevitably would, I whispered into her ear, "I'm here for you. I know it's hard, but you can trust me. Tell me what's bothering you, or don't. I won't put any pressure on you, but if you think it will help then I'm listening."

Bonnie eased away and wiped her eyes, then smiled up at me, a glimmer of renewed faith in the kindness of people clear to see, and said, "Melody is as much a daughter to Del as me. Maybe more so. She spent so much time with him, and I worry that maybe he changed his will and left the shop to her and she killed him once she knew he'd done it. It's awful, and I'm a despicable person for thinking such things, but I can't shake this terrible feeling inside. I'm not normally like this, Max, I promise you, but I keep thinking spiteful, cruel things about everyone. Even my own husband. Isn't that the worst?"

"Bonnie, let me tell you something, and I hope that you're up to listening properly. Are you?"

Bonnie nodded. "I am."

"Then here's the truth of it, and it's something I've learned the hard way. You can't always trust your own thoughts. Sometimes, your mind is not your friend. Things go around and around and you imagine these scenarios that haven't even happened, or you fixate on the past, and replay events over and over. You think you're in control, but if you stop and watch your thoughts you realise that sometimes, and more often than you'd believe, your mind is your enemy. You have to be alert, watch what you think, and let go of the past as it's done. Try not to imagine the future, but rather live in the present and stop those bad vibes in their tracks. Sorry, does that sound flaky? Too much like I'm going to tell you to go on a meditation retreat to find yourself?"

"No! Oh, Max, you're absolutely right! It's like my head is conspiring against me and the thoughts won't stop. That was exactly what I needed. To accept that sometimes what you think isn't even really you, but just your brain turning to the dark side and putting these things in your head whether you want them there or not."

"And although it isn't easy to stop them, you can. You tell them that's not what you want to think, that it isn't helping, and you turn your attention to something positive, something good. Like the memories you have of Del, the legacy he left. That's better, right?"

"Absolutely. Thank you, Max. Thank you so much." Bonnie stood on tiptoe, brushed her dark hair from her face, and beamed at me before kissing my cheek.

"Now, how about a coffee? I've got a pot of the nice stuff and it's still hot, so let's get lazy Melody up and we can decide what's going to happen today. Sound good?"

"It sounds perfect."

As we wandered back to the van, my heart skipping a beat as I looked at the awesome gazebo, my amazing home on wheels, and the kitchen arrangement, Melody appeared in the doorway, then hopped down and yawned as she stretched her arms to the sky. She was tousled from sleep, hair wild, but probably the prettiest she'd ever looked. I knew in my heart that she was a good person.

Bonnie had let her thoughts get the better of her, which was understandable and completely normal, but from the way her shoulders relaxed and a genuine smile spread across her face, I knew she trusted Melody too. The emotional turmoil she was experiencing meant of course she wouldn't know what was what, even making her question those she trusted most in the world.

"Morning," I called out as Melody spotted us.

"Gosh, what time is it? I feel like I slept for ages. Vee is such a nice camper, Max, and that weird bed was super comfortable."

"Really? When I slept in it, my legs hung off the end and I kept feeling like I was in a coffin."

"But you still offered to sleep in it? What a gentleman. Hey, Bonnie, what are you doing here? Couldn't sleep, eh?" Her smile faded, replaced with sympathy.

"The girls were up at the crack of dawn and wanted to come and see what happened last night. They miss their Grampy and didn't want to stay at home. Maybe we should have stayed last night."

"It got quite rowdy." Melody stifled another yawn, then sniffed, her eyes drawn to the coffee pot. "Oh, Max, you're a star. Can I have a cup?"

"Let's all have one, and we can discuss what's happening today."

I poured coffees and arranged chairs, then we sat and watched the girls race after Anxious who was desperately trying to find a place to hide but was out of time before he had the chance. They'd hit it off so well, and the distraction for the twins gave Bonnie some breathing space.

"Melody, I have an admission to make," stuttered Bonnie, hiding her shame behind her raised mug.

"Don't tell me," she chuckled, although her mood wasn't overtly jovial, "you've begun to doubt everything you think you know and suspect everyone, including me, of killing Del?"

"How did you know?"

"Because I've been doing the exact same thing. I even thought it might be you to claim the inheritance."

"And I worried Dad had changed his will and you'd inherit the shop and you got rid of him because of that. I'm so sorry, and of course I don't believe it. Max set me straight, and I'm so grateful you're here, Max. Melody, I know we aren't the closest, but I do think of you as a friend, and you have done so much for our family. I know Dad loved you, and would never have managed without your help, so please forgive me?"

"There's nothing to forgive. We're good, Bonnie, honestly. Don't give it a second thought."

"Then it's settled," sighed Bonnie. "The one thing we do know is that us three are innocent. Everyone else is a suspect."

We laughed at the absurdity of the situation, knowing that somewhere out there the true killer was hiding, and maybe in plain sight. They knew much better than me who that might be, but so far neither had come up with a name, nor had anyone in mind we might question with a motive, because Del was simply a fine man with no enemies. Was that really true, or was he like so many others I'd encountered and had a terrible secret he'd been hiding that had eventually meant he'd been killed because of it?

"I was thinking maybe we should return to the shop today?" I suggested. "Ensure everything is as it should be, go over things yet again, and maybe something will turn up. What do you think?"

"That's not a bad idea," agreed Melody. "I need to get home to shower and change first, as that is the one downside to vanlife, Max. How do you manage?"

"I usually use campsite facilities, or used to, but I got a gym membership and there's one nearby, so I might use that, have a swim, maybe even a sauna, then I could meet you later."

"You're welcome to shower at mine."

"Or mine," said Bonnie. "It's the least I could do."

"Thank you both, but I'd like to have a workout anyway. Bonnie, are you free today?"

"Not until much later. I have to see the solicitor, and there's a mountain of paperwork to begin, let alone the funeral to arrange and so many other things my head is spinning."

"I can help with some of that this morning," said Melody, "then we can meet Max at the shop after lunch or I can if it's too much."

"Would you mind going without me? I need time to think, and the girls have had enough upset. I'll do something nice with them later on once we get some things arranged."

We agreed that would be fine, so once we'd finished our drinks, we called for Anxious and the girls. All three were beyond excited, eyes wild with the thrill of the game and the chance to let loose, and wanted to continue playing. Bonnie explained there were things that had to be done, so we said goodbye and everyone left, leaving Anxious and I to clear up the kitchen after breakfast and enjoy the solitude after so much activity since arriving only yesterday morning but felt like days ago.

After relaxing to gather our thoughts, we headed to the gym, the gift of a membership from my parents a real help since Christmas, and today I planned to use the facilities and make the most of it.

Chapter 14

The workout was awesome. I pushed hard with the free weights, a treat after last year involving a bodyweight workout most mornings, then used several machines for a killer leg workout too. I was tired but jubilant by the end, and keening for what came next. Knowing I had as much time as I wanted, as it was still only early and there were hours before I met Melody, I took a long, incredibly hot shower. The gym chain was known for its luxurious showers and it did not disappoint. Next I went into the sauna and sweated out the toxins, alternating between a cold rinse and the steamy goodness, back and forth until my skin was aglow and the good hormones were raging through my system.

What was even better about the whole experience was that as it was mid-morning I had the entire sauna to myself. I could pour water on the rocks and increase the temperature whenever I wished without having to ask anyone. It was truly divine.

What made the whole thing extra special, and it meant I could use the various gyms throughout the country at any time of year, was the doggie day care they offered as part of the package. It was a real pooch party, and proof that my folks had really thought through the gift.

Anxious adored our regular trips to the various locations, as it was more like kindergarten than kennels, with keen young men and women eager to give the little guy the adoration he believed was his birthright. Walks around the extensive grounds, treats, cuddles, and the chance to play with other dogs in a secret compound meant he liked the gym as much as me.

I sat, smiling at the thought of him lording it up while I baked in my own sweat on a towel, a bizarre thing if you thought about it too much, but one that worked wonders on the mind and body. I glanced up and smiled as a man entered, thankfully keeping his towel wrapped around his waist as he sat on the pine slatted bench opposite. I thought I recognised him, but wasn't sure where from, but assumed he was a face around the town.

"Hi," he said.

"Hi. Been for a swim or a workout?"

"Look at me, and tell me which one you think," he laughed.

"Okay, you're on. Hairy, including your back, not much hair on top, big beard, slightly overweight if it's okay to say so," he nodded it was, as there was no denying it, "but you're fit and move well. You're a lane swimmer. One of the guys who does lap after lap without ever seeming to tire. What's your secret?"

"Spot on!" he chuckled. "I know I'm rather a cliché. You see guys like me up and down the country. For some reason, and don't ask me why, the hairier the back, the more likely the bloke is to be doing lengths. I come most days, then hit the sauna. Makes you feel alive, doesn't it?"

"It sure does. Have I seen you around town?"

"You don't recognise me, do you?"

"Sorry, but no."

"I was in the pub yesterday, reading the paper, when you came in to have a word with old Charlie. Bet he gave you the right run around, didn't he? Man likes to gossip, but don't pay him too much attention. He's what you'd call a slight exaggerator if you were being kind. If you weren't, there are plenty more choice words to describe the daft old duffer. A pain in the rear being one of them."

"Not a fan then?

"He's fine enough in small doses. I grew up here, like him, and we're about the same age give or take a few years, but I don't have much time for the likes of Charlie. I get my milk, but don't chat much unless he corners me."

"Charlie was polite enough. He did seem to enjoy gossiping, but actually that was what I was after."

"Ah yes, the famous amateur sleuth embroiled in another mystery. Don't worry, I haven't been looking you up or anything, but I heard all about our new arrival. You, along with poor Del's murder, are the talk of the town. Everyone loves to natter around here, especially if it's a tall, dark stranger riding into town in his cool VW."

"You're a campervan fan?"

"Me? Nah, not my thing, mate. Strictly a homebody. The wife takes care of me and in return I try not to get under her feet. Which is why I come here most days. She enjoys her space, and I do, too, so it is what it is and I'm happy about that."

"I'm Max." I reached forward and we shook.

"Tom. Nice to meet you. So, ask away." Tom grinned, waiting for my questions, and no way was I going to pass up the opportunity to talk with another resident.

"Is there anything you want to tell me? Anything at all about Del and what happened? How much do you know?"

Tom shifted his position, leaning forward as if ready to conspire, then admitted, "I do have a few things you might like to hear. First, what have you been told about Charlie?"

"Not much. Just that he's a gossip and knows everything that goes on."

"But do you know that he was fiddling the milk and he and Del had a right old argument last week? I mean, epic."

"I did not know that. Melody never said, and she seems to know him quite well. Surely Del would have told her?"

"I guess not. That wasn't Del's way, and he would never badmouth someone, even to Melody, as he always allowed people to make up their own minds about others. He had a true heart of gold, that man, and he'll be sorely missed."

"Everyone says the same. So, what's this about an argument over milk? How do you even fiddle the milk? And how do you know they argued?"

"I know because I was there. Right in the pub beer garden, it was. Del made an infrequent stop off for a pint and when he clocked Charlie, they went at it hell for leather. They were lucky nobody else was there to hear what Del had to say, and Charlie admitting what he'd done. Terrible business."

"Over milk? I guess people have fallen out over less."

"True. Anyway, I was tucked around the corner nursing my beer, keeping to myself and reading the paper, when I heard it kick off. They didn't know I was there. Del confronted Charlie, said the milk must be off because it was messing with his pastry and things weren't turning out right."

"Like a soggy bottom with his quiche?" I mused, wondering if that was the issue.

"I wouldn't know about that. Charlie said Del was being dumb as his milk was the same as always and from just up the road from the dairy. Del insisted something wasn't right, then he threatened to report Charlie for it and Del knew everyone, including Charlie's boss, who wouldn't take kindly to the idea of tampering. Charlie caved and admitted that he'd been watering it down on occasion. Not always, but sometimes, and nobody had noticed."

"Why bother? That's a lot of effort to save a few pennies."

"The pennies add up to pounds, and Charlie is always hard up. Spends too much on beer. He admitted as much to Del, said times were hard, and all he did was water it down sometimes, and only recently, so he could sell more. I don't like to say who he sold the extra to, but I bet you have your suspicions now."

"Let me guess. Constance from the pastry shop?"

"You got it! Charlie said she gave him a great price because he was creaming off the cream if you get me, so she got not only milk, but the really rich stuff which everyone knows is the best on your cereal of a morning. I guess she used it for her baking or something. That world eludes me, I'm afraid to say."

"So Charlie was earning a few extra pounds by messing with the milk and got found out by Del? Did he promise to stop?"

"He absolutely did, and I don't think Charlie was the kind of guy to risk it again. He needs his job, and was lucky Del didn't report him. I never told anyone as it was just a dumb thing, but maybe I should have spoken up. Think old Charlie offed Del as he was worried about getting fired? Should I tell the police?"

"You could call them and ask for the detectives running the case and let them know, but it's most likely unrelated. If it salves your conscience, though, then sure, tell them."

"Max, I think I will. Actually, it's a relief to tell someone. It's been bugging me, you know, so thanks for asking."

"I'm glad you told me. I'm surprised Charlie would take such a risk, especially with loyal customers, but at least he stopped."

"I'm guessing he started with the skimmed milk as who would notice the difference, then realised he could earn more if he siphoned off the full fat milk. Cheeky bugger, right?"

"Absolutely. Nice to meet you, Tom. And I appreciate the heads-up." We shook again, then I left, had a cold shower, then couldn't resist and had a warm one, too, feeling so clean I wondered if I'd removed a few layers of skin.

After collecting Anxious, who was absolutely exhausted after so much playing, I nipped back to the airfield, sorted out some clothes, put towels and whatnot out to dry as the weather was decent enough although not exactly boiling, then had a light lunch before heading back into town again to meet Melody at the deli and see what we could uncover.

Things were coming together. I could feel it more after my relaxing morning, with various bits of information sorting themselves in my subconscious, ready to become a cohesive whole and let me figure this thing out. Not that I would mind if the DIs solved it first, or anyone else for that matter, as the main thing was that Del's killer was brought to justice.

It would be nice if I figured it out though! I didn't mind admitting that.

The milk float trundled along the high street, people smiling as they waved at Charlie, the old-fashioned vehicle from a bygone era eliciting memories from those of a certain generation, confused looks from those too young to recall such a once daily sight.

Charlie was in his element, waving at the children, tapping his hat to the adults as he crept along, stopping occasionally to deliver what I assumed were extra orders. Would this man have murdered over milk? Worried he'd be uncovered and lose his job? He'd done it for decades, so that must have been a real concern, as his whole identity was that of jovial milkman. The fact he wore his uniform out of work hours proof it was a major part of his life.

I nodded as he passed us, and he tipped his cap and smiled, a frown creasing his already lined face before he was past us, continuing his 4 mph dash, the empty bottles rattling in their crates.

For a Tuesday, the town was busy, with people browsing shop windows, in and out of the newsagents and the bakery, the butchers packed with locals. Tourists were in evidence, a surefire indicator of the encroaching warmer weather and longer days when those who had the luxury would come to visit whilst others were working so they weren't battling over car park spaces or having to wait so long at cafes.

With so many great walks and sites of interest close by, Welshpool and Newtown were the perfect destinations as starting points for trips to Montgomery castle or strolls along the canal, with plenty of stop-offs at the bustling pubs along the way. Not to mention the garden centres, where spring stock would now be for sale, the larger ones doing as much business in the restaurants and gift shops as they did by selling plants.

I missed having a garden and sitting at the table with a cup of coffee in the morning, listening to the birds, laughing and joking with Min, but when I really thought about it, when was the last time that had actually happened? For years before we divorced, my mind would be elsewhere, stressing over menus, devising new ones, my thoughts dark and angry when I dwelt on whatever nonsense had happened in the restaurant that week. None of it was important, I'd simply chosen to let it affect me, to consume all my waking hours, when I should have been paying attention to the beautiful, caring woman sat opposite me, a sad, faraway look on her face as she lamented the loss of the man she'd married.

How had I not seen the signs? How had I let it go so far and get so out of hand that she had no choice but to ask for a divorce? What a fool I'd been.

"Complete idiot, more like," I mumbled, shaking my head in wonder at the man I'd become, yet pleased that I'd managed to change. To become a better human being, and to perform a much overdue overhaul of my attitude and what I deemed important.

"Excuse me?" snapped Constance, whirling on me from her position outside the deli where she'd had her face to the glass, her hands cupped either side to block the light and see inside.

"Sorry, I was miles away and talking to myself. I was reminiscing about not having a garden and how I used to sit outside and enjoy the bird chatter. Somehow, I lost that calmness and can't even recall when I last did it back then and was actually living in the moment and enjoying what was right in front of me." I smiled sheepishly, aware I was sharing too much with someone who was basically a stranger.

"Oh, you're one of those," said Constance, shaking her head.

"One of what?"

"Someone who thinks they can change, become a different person."

"I have changed. I am different. I'm still me, but I think about what I'm doing, how I act, and make adjustments if needed."

"Nonsense!" she hissed. "People are just people, and some are obsessive, others don't care about much at all. Max, you like everything to be perfect, just like me. We have passion, get consumed by it, and there is absolutely nothing wrong with that."

"Not even if it's to the detriment of those around you? People you love?"

"Not even then. We have to do what feels right, what calls us, and having a deep passion, maybe an obsession if you'd like to call it that, is a wonderful thing. It means at least we care deeply about something."

"I disagree. Sure, you can have something that you focus on and work hard at, but if it interferes with what's truly important, which is being happy, then is it worth the sacrifice? I think not, but that's only my opinion."

"And look where it's got you. Talking to a stranger in a small town, with no home, no wife, no garden you say you miss, and investigating a stranger's death. Call that things working out?" She sneered, her mouth set in a sour line of distaste.

"What about you, Constance? Are you happy? Do you have what you want out of life?"

"Don't be ridiculous! Who's happy? Properly happy, I mean? Nobody, that's who. I have no partner, I live alone, I work incredibly long hours, and have no real friends."

"So what's the point?" I was genuinely intrigued by this woman, and wondered what it was that kept her going.

"Because I adore running my shop. It's my life, like it was Del's, and nobody is going to take it away from me. Look what happened to him because he got lax, slacked off, lost his mojo. He could have been big, had multiple shops all over the country, but no, he eased off right when he should have knuckled down and redoubled his efforts."

"But life changes, and Del's did. He realised that family was more important, and as the twins got older, he spent more time with them. He still worked very hard, but he made sure to spend time with his family too. According to Melody and Bonnie, that's what gave him even more joy than the deli."

"Utter rubbish! They'll get older, leave this place, and he would hardly have seen them. Then what?"

"That's a very cynical way to look at things, if you don't mind me saying."

"I do not mind. I do what I want and answer to nobody. My shop is the best in the area. Everyone says so."

"So it's a matter of pride? But who really cares, apart from you? What do you want from life, Constance?"

"To not be asked dumb questions!" Constance turned from me and stood back on the pavement to study the shop frontage, and shook her head. "He could have done so much more."

"He was getting older, and didn't want more on his plate. He was happy, by all accounts, and was enjoying his life, his shop and work, but other things too."

"I want it."

"Want what?"

"The shop. It's no accident he died now, right when he was slacking off. You wouldn't get me to let someone murder me in my own shop. I'd see them coming a mile off and never let them get me. I bet the old fool fell over and did it to himself."

Her words hit home in a way I hadn't expected, and the back of my neck tingled. She wasn't right, but then again, maybe she was.

Chapter 15

The shop door unlocked and Melody stepped outside, a smile for me, a vicious scowl for Constance who was glaring at Melody like she's just dissed her sausage rolls, taunted her quiche, and mocked her pies.

"It's you," snarled Melody.

"And you," snapped Constance.

"What's going on? Why are you two looking like you're about to punch each other?"

Anxious, who had kept quiet until now, clearly not interested in Constance, barked at Melody and wagged his tail, breaking the stand-off.

"Oh, sorry, Anxious. How are you doing?" Melody kept her eyes on Constance as she fussed over the little guy who rubbed against her leg happily then barked again, this time at the rival shop owner.

"What's up, buddy?" I asked. "Something you want to say?"

"He can't understand you," sighed Constance, tutting in a condescending manner that got all our hackles raised.

"Sometimes he understands more than humans," I explained. "Right now, he's saying you have something else to say. What is it?"

Anxious sat, head cocked, focus on her as Melody and I exchanged a glance.

"If you must know, I came to speak to Bonnie, but it can wait."

"Bonnie isn't here. She's spending time with the twins." Melody turned to go back inside, but Constance took hold of her upper arm and yanked her back sharply.

"Then you'll have to do. Tell Bonnie that I'm interested in the shop. If she inherits, then I'd like to buy it from her. I'll give a good price, but I want to keep the name."

"You dare come around here the day after Del was murdered and ask about buying the business?" hissed Melody, eyes wide with surprise that quickly flashed with anger.

"The vultures will be circling soon enough, especially the supermarket chains or a coffee shop conglomerate. We've got enough of those already, and if we aren't careful there won't be any more independent businesses left. The high street is already dying, and people want local enterprise run by real people, not those faceless corporations."

"I know all that! What's that got to do with anything?"

"Because they'll want to destroy the business, turn it into something awful, and I won't have it. Tell Bonnie to speak to me first before they convince her to sell. I can't offer what they will, but it will be a fair price. I want this business. People liked the deli, and I want the shop and the name. I have big plans, and I want to combine the deli side of things with my pastry. It will be huge."

I frowned, then asked, "So, what you're saying is that you want to build up a chain of shops using yours and Del's businesses? How is that different from what you said you don't want to happen?"

"Because it will be done properly and nothing like those faceless, horrible places. It will be for local people, which I am, with local produce. Not stuff from the other side of the country or beyond."

"I'll pass on the message. Did you ever make this offer to Del?" asked Melody, planting her feet wide as if ready to fight if Constance started anything. You could cut the air with a knife, the tension was so high.

"What if I did? I spoke to him the other day about it, if you must know. It's not a secret. Surely he told you?" Constance sneered, pleased to get one over on Melody, as it was clear he hadn't mentioned it.

"He never said a word, but that's because he would never sell. Probably didn't even think it was worth mentioning."

"That's where you're wrong!" Constance laughed, an utterly forced, spiteful guffaw. "I made him a great offer, and he was surprised by it. Said it would solve all his problems and he could go on an incredible adventure with the twins."

"Liar! He wouldn't do that. How could he go on an adventure with them? They have school. They live with their parents. He couldn't just take them off and leave all this behind."

"Then why don't you ask him?" hissed Constance. The moment the words were spoken her eyes widened, she opened and closed her mouth like a landed fish, and her neck flushed.

The silence stretched out as Melody turned bright red, her fists clenched, then she slapped Constance hard across the cheek, the *crack* almost as loud as the women's gasps of shock.

"I... I'm so sorry," stammered Melody. "I shouldn't have done that. It was wrong. You got me riled up, as you're so mean, but that was uncalled for. Violence is never the answer, no matter how much the other deserves it."

"No, you were right to do it. I spoke out of turn and that was a horrid thing to say." Constance's hand went to her cheek, the red mark clearly sore. "Of course he would never take the twins without their parents say-so, and I know how much you cared for him. I should never have said such a mean thing. I apologise."

"So do I. Did he consider your offer? Really?"

"Not really, no. He said it would be great to have the extra money to do something with the twins, but he didn't mean take them away. He loved them so much. Doted on the sweet children. But he turned me down, said he could never leave the shop, that he wouldn't know what to do with himself without it. We were more alike than you will ever know, Melody. We both lived to see the smiles on the faces of our customers, knowing we'd done our all to give them the absolute best. Max seems to think I should forget about it and take up knitting. He doesn't understand."

"You're twisting my words. That isn't what I said at all. Working hard, taking pride in your business, is admirable. What I said was that if you become so obsessed that you neglect everything else, then you need to take a long, hard look in the mirror. Del always had time for his family, by all accounts, so he had the right balance."

"He would never put the shop before them," agreed Melody. Ignoring Constance, she asked me, "Are you coming in?"

"Yes. Goodbye, Constance."

"Goodbye." She turned on her heels, and with a backwards glare at us, she clattered down the high street, her red shoes flashing in the sunshine.

"How does she stand all day in those?" I wondered.

"She doesn't. When she's behind the counter, she puts on her trainers, but when she's out and about, she gets changed. It's always about appearances with that woman."

We entered the shop then Melody locked the door, and both of us took a deep breath then smiled at each other.

"She's intense," I said.

"She sure is. Has a nasty streak, too, but I should never have slapped her. Now she has something on me, and that's never good. I can't believe her though. Trying to take over before Del's even cold. Terrible."

"She's definitely trying to take advantage, but don't let it concern you. Bonnie wouldn't sell, would she?"

"I don't know. She hasn't got the time to run this place, and has plenty to deal with already. Who knows what will happen now?"

"Shall we take another look around? See if we missed anything? I know we've already done that, but it can't hurt, can it?"

"That's why we're both here, so let's get busy."

For the next hour, we wandered around the shop, checked the office, the storage rooms, the kitchen, then found ourselves in the alley with nothing gained from our search apart from a sense of emptiness. The place felt like it had lost its soul. No customers, no smells of fresh food, a quiet kitchen without the clattering of pots and pans, no deliveries or ringing of the old-fashioned till meant it felt less like a bustling local shop and more like a mausoleum.

"I can't stand it in there now," said Melody. "Without Del, it's like the place has died too. What am I going to do? How will we ever figure this out?"

"We're getting there, I'm sure of it." I explained about my conversation with Constance before the slap incident, and what I'd learned about Charlie and his milk thievery, her eyes bugging as I told the tale.

"The sneaky bugger! I always knew he was a bit dodgy, but nobbling the milk? That's awful."

"It is, but what's more important is that Del threatened to report him. Charlie lives for his job, and that was a serious threat hanging over him. It seems far-fetched, but could this really be over watery milk? I had another mystery last year that seemed to hinge on the milk for an ice-cream shop, and that didn't end well."

"It can't be that. Charlie might be a chancer, and a terrible gossip, but to commit murder? No, I can't see it."

"Then let's see if we can retrace Del's steps, play out a few different scenarios, and see if anything sparks an idea. It's worth a shot."

"We have nothing to lose."

With Anxious watching in confused silence, we both took turns pretending to be Del, going back into the office, writing the letter, then going out into the alley and acting like the killer was there. Whichever way we played it, it made no sense, as either Del had been forced to write the note by the killer, which was beyond unlikely, or he knew what was about happen yet still went into the alley to meet his demise.

Once we'd finished playing out every scenario we could imagine, we stood where he'd been found and I said, "None of that could have happened. It doesn't feel right."

"Then what does feel right? I can't figure this out at all. Sure, the stabbing part is obvious, but with the note and his attitude about the quiche being so jokey, it doesn't add up."

"Then that's our answer! And why didn't we see it all along?"

"Max, you've lost me."

"If it makes no sense, absolutely doesn't add up, then that's because it never happened. This didn't happen. Del wasn't murdered. He wrote the note, that's a given, but he wasn't expecting to die for real."

"Then why did he write it? Why involve you? And unless I'm mistaken, he was stabbed."

"Or was he?"

"Max, there was a bloody big and apparently expensive knife in his throat. Of course he was stabbed."

I breathed deeply, gathered my thoughts, and said, "He couldn't have been murdered. Nobody writes a message like that then goes to their death. The killer wouldn't allow it, and he wouldn't have stood by to be killed. We should have been looking at this a different way all along. I can't believe we didn't see it right from the start. Or the detectives."

"And what way should we be looking at this?"

"Del was convinced he was playing a game. A strange, and as yet unexplained game, but that was all this was.

Something went horribly wrong, but he never for one moment believed he was about to be murdered."

"So he was with someone, they were messing around, then that person stabbed him?"

"Not that either. I don't think there was anyone else here at all. Come on, let me show you."

With no way of knowing exactly what occurred, I nevertheless showed Melody my working hypothesis, which took mere moments, and she agreed that it was a possibility, but nothing more. It still didn't explain the rest of this puzzling conundrum, but we still had people to talk to and other avenues to investigate, so we decided to keep digging and doing what we could to honour Del's memory and get him the justice he deserved, if, indeed, there was justice to be served.

As we discussed all possibilities further, it became more and more apparent to me that we had been barking up the wrong tree and what everyone had thought happened actually hadn't.

Focused on Del's cryptic message, things had been overlooked, and it was easy to understand why. We came up with a plan of sorts, very rudimentary, and after ironing out the finer details, and reminding each other that we had to tread very carefully indeed with this, I went into the shop and made a call to the DIs to explain what I believed had happened. Feeling strangely nervous, I asked permission to deal with it in the way Melody and I thought best. Whether we were right or not, only time would tell, but the more I talked, the more convinced I was of what really happened.

It was a difficult conversation, with Laura and Bishop bickering on speakerphone, until finally they agreed to let us handle things as long as we promised to remain safe and that those involved would be made to confess. It wasn't a promise I could guarantee, but I told them I would do my best, then hung up and turned to find Anxious staring at me in his usual inquisitive way.

"Don't look at me like that. What else can I do? If what I think happened actually did, then this is for the best for everyone. If you have a better idea, I'm all ears." I paused, but the pooch simply stared at me. "No, didn't think so." I stroked his head and he barked that he'd go along with the plan, but only under sufferance, and I supposed that was fair enough.

Melody and I discussed things further, then she locked up the deli and we wandered along the high street, both feeling rather apprehensive, and uncertain if how we'd decided to handle this was actually the best way. We went over our options, returning to the original plan eventually, as it seemed like the safest and least stressful way to handle it for everyone involved.

With a few hours until it was time to act, beyond Melody making a phone call and arranging things, we parted ways. We would meet later, but until then there were other matters on my mind that I wanted to clear up.

First, I went to the pub and found Charlie in his usual spot, unsurprised to find him alone. I popped inside, got him a beer, but stuck to a soda water for myself, then returned outside and asked if I could join him.

"Suit yourself," he grunted, clearly surprised by my request, pleased about the beer. "Thanks," he said with a nod as I slid the pint across the picnic table.

"No problem. So, let's get this over with. You were out for Del, weren't you?"

"What!?" he spluttered, spitting beer everywhere. "Get lost. I don't have to listen to such nonsense from a stranger. What's your game, eh?"

"No game, just after the truth. You were trying to ruin him in your own rather ridiculous way. Little things, like messing with the milk, watering it down so his cooking suffered, but it was more than that, wasn't it?"

"I don't know what you're talking about. Charlie glanced around, worried someone might hear, but we were alone outside so he bent close, sneered, and hissed, "Prove it. There's nothing to be said about it, and it's over anyway. Next, you'll be saying I murdered him."

"Did you?" I taunted, keen to see his reaction.

It was one of utter panic. "Look, bigshot detective who isn't really one, I admit to watering down the milk, but I don't do that anymore and what business is it of yours?"

"It involves Del, so it's my business. I promised the family, and Melody, I'd help. That's what I'm doing."

"Seems to me you're sticking your nose in where it isn't wanted or needed. Leave the professionals to do their job. I liked Del, and I don't care if you believe that or not, but times are tough and a man has to do what a man has to do to survive. I've been at this game for decades and look where it's got me. Absolutely nowhere! Leave me be."

"In a few minutes, I will, but I want the truth first."

"There's nothing to tell. All I've ever done is put in a good word for Constance, encourage the locals to use her shop rather than Del's. She paid me to do it, but that's just business."

"Nothing else? No fights with him?"

"Yeah, we had an argument about the milk, but that was it. How'd you know about that?"

"I just do. So what was your arrangement with Constance? And I hope it won't happen again."

"How can it? He's dead."

"If the shop opens again with Bonnie in charge, I hope you won't interfere."

"Too right I won't. That daft woman, Constance, never even paid me. Laughed when I said I'd done what she asked and tried to spread the word that her shop was better. It didn't work anyway, and believe it or not, I felt bad for doing it. Del was a kind soul and a much better man than me. I've known him for decades. Not like that stuck-up newcomer."

"That's all I wanted to hear." With a nod, and a yip of disappointment from Anxious, we left Charlie to his pint and retreated to Vee.

It was time to return to the airfield and put an end to this very perplexing mystery.

First, I had a stop to make.

Chapter 16

I felt like a pervert, a sneak, a voyeur as I pulled up at the far end of the road and located Bonnie's house by the number Melody had given me. It was a nice place, your typical suburban detached home where the front gardens were a mix of well-manicured lawns, narrow flower beds, and tarmac drives leading to garages no doubt stuffed with items that couldn't fit in the houses, having never had a car in them since they were first built.

It felt strange being on a regular street where regular people went about regular lives, as once this had been me, although we did have a larger house with all the trappings of wealth I'd thought would make me happy but did the opposite. It felt like lifetimes ago now, but I wanted to see, to know I was heading down the right path with not only this particular mystery but my own life too.

It took no longer than the time to turn off the engine to be sure I had made the right decision by leaving it behind. Sure, it had taken Min's massive decision to file for divorce for me to get the wake-up call. Without it, I might have continued doing what I'd always done and obsess over work, strive to be the best even though I knew in my heart it wasn't good for my mental health or my home life.

But I hadn't. I'd changed. Done what was needed to get myself on the right path, even though to everyone else it seemed like madness at the time. Now I was part of a community many didn't even know existed, or not on the scale it did. Hundreds of thousands of people living in campervans, motorhomes, even cars. Some out of choice because of the freedom it afforded, others because of necessity whether they liked it or not.

I knew I was beyond lucky to have the choice, could settle back into a house if I so chose, but I wouldn't do that unless Min insisted. Not that I would hold it against her, as everyone is different, but I got the impression she would join me on the vagabond trip when the time came—I longed for it so much that it made my heart actually hurt.

Watching Bonnie's house like a sneak made it all the more real. That there was an opportunity to live how she did, with her family in their nice house, plush carpets, a garden, big TV, kitchen in a proper room not under a gazebo. But I wasn't jealous. I was reassured that it was no longer for me.

The twins came out of the front door, chatting quietly to each other, their movements slow. They picked up their scooters from the drive, then slowly rode them around and around, talking now and then, but mostly silent. It must have hit them so hard knowing Del was gone, but at least they had each other to talk to.

Bonnie appeared, talking with a man I assumed was her husband, Tony. A white Ford Transit Connect was in the drive, with a business name and number on the side, so he was probably between road assistance jobs. Working for a small, private company would mean he would come and go at all hours. It was good he was here with her now, and I hoped he'd been helping her sort out things, although I knew Melody had helped her this morning too.

Tony was a solid man with a kind face, a baseball cap over short hair, and sported a simple outfit of jeans and T-shirt hugging his muscular frame. They held hands as they watched the children play, calling out now and then to encourage them to try their bunny hops again, the twins excited for a few minutes and laughing before the loss hit them again and they resumed their monotonous circuits.

Nobody had spoken much about Bonnie's husband, but from what little had been said it was to extol his virtues as a good husband, but that he spent a lot of time away from home and kept very irregular hours because of his job. All to provide for his family, or was it because home life wasn't as perfect as he'd envisioned and he used work as an excuse? It happened, I knew it did, but nobody had even hinted that was the case here.

I still wanted to see for myself, just to get as clear a picture as I could of the family before I dropped a bombshell on them when they were already grieving and Bonnie was trying to organise what came next.

I'd seen enough, but didn't want to let them notice me as what would they think then? Itching to get away, but staying low in my seat, I remained until they went inside, then drove off back to the campsite feeling heavy of heart and like I was about to ruin what little remained of their happy home life. It would be for the best, I was sure of that, but it was still a lot to take on, and different from how these things usually played out.

To keep myself busy, I re-arranged things in Vee, perfecting my organisational skills, going over the small cupboards and drawers and the garage area, deciding to get rid of several items I never used, making a list of things I needed to get instead, a little flutter of excitement as I anticipated a shopping trip. That would be a rare treat, as when you had nowhere to put stuff you couldn't just buy whatever you fancied as what would be the point?

With a while to wait until events came to a head, I called for Anxious and we went for a wander. The airfield was massive, and I was yet to do a full circuit in daylight. I'd walked it last night when the party was in full swing, which was an event I will always remember, but that was more of a meandering vigil rather than circumnavigating the entire site.

Anxious skipped ahead, not a care in the world, lighting up my life like he always did. Who couldn't help smiling at his antics as he raced about, sniffing trails, going up to complete strangers and lifting his paw to elicit the usual "Aw," before taking whatever treat was offered and hurrying away as they called out, "Hey, what about your poorly paw?"

I chatted with a few people, swapping vanlife tips, picking up a few wayward wrappers because of the wind, but the site was incredibly tidy and everyone was doing their bit to keep it litter free. It lifted my spirits no end to know that people cared about their environment and tried to leave no trace when they inevitably moved on, although I did meet a few who had been in the same spot for months and had no intention of leaving.

When we arrived back at the pitch, it was to find an unexpected guest.

"Veronica, what are you doing here?"

She shifted from one leg to the other, eyes downcast then drifting to Vee. "Nice campervan. Max, can I ask you a question?"

"Sure. Would you like to sit, or have a drink?"

"No thank you. You were expecting me, I assume?"

"What gives you that idea?"

"Because of everything that happened. Del's death. The suspicious circumstances. I know about your wiki page, someone told me, and the way you've been asking questions around town I assume you'd come and see me again or think I'd visit you."

"Take a seat, Veronica. I don't know what you've heard, but yes, I'm looking into Del's death because of certain things that happened. You knew him better than you let on, didn't you?"

"Nobody knew, and I thought I could keep it that way. Now I'm not so sure. Max, you have to believe me that I didn't do it." Veronica glanced at the chair then slumped into it, her hands tapping her thighs to a rhythm only she could hear.

"Why come here? I haven't asked you about it, and it's none of my business. Maybe I would have in time, but something's happened, so I think it's best left alone now. Am I wrong?"

"Maybe. Oh, I don't know!"

"Why are you so worried?" I took a seat beside her and looked into her eyes. A tear ran down her cheek.

"Because I loved him. There, I said it. I loved the daft old man and his obsession with that damn deli. You bringing the food almost broke me. It was the last time I'd ever see one of his stupid quiches again. He so loved his quiche!"

"I had my suspicions that you two were an item, but what I don't get is why keep it a secret? Surely there was nothing to be ashamed of? Bonnie would have been all for it, wouldn't she? Her dad getting a second chance at things? He deserved it."

"He was a very private man, and you need to be in a place like this unless you want everyone talking about you behind your back. We both agreed to keep our relationship to ourselves until we knew for certain where it was headed, if anywhere, and now it's too late for me to tell him how I feel. I loved him, and if I'd told him maybe things would have been different. I was worried it was too much, too soon, but now I wonder if he might still be alive if I'd let my feelings be known."

"I don't think it would have changed anything. Your relationship has nothing to do with how, or why, he died."

"Are you sure?" Veronica wiped her eyes and looked into mine with hope.

"Of course. Was it the quiche? Is that why you thought it had something to do with you? I thought it might. When I mentioned the soggy bottom you became tearful, which I thought strange, but I figured that was your business. Private, and not relevant to what happened."

"You didn't tell the police?"

"No."

"Maybe you should have."

"I assumed you would have told them you two were an item if you thought it would help them to figure this out. Maybe I was wrong. Seeing how you reacted, and how nobody else knew about it, made me believe that it was early days and I wasn't even sure if anything was going on at all. Just a hunch. I was more concerned about the food being poisoned."

"You're a kind man, Max Effort. Too kind and trusting, if anything. Del and I had flirted for years, just silly stuff, and then a few weeks ago we spent the evening talking and we went on a few dates after that. We clicked, and I know he felt it too. That was it, and nothing ever happened, but I think we could both see where it was headed, so took it slowly. Del had been on his own for so many years, so have I, so neither of us wanted to rush into things. Maybe we were too cautious."

"Veronica, it's fine. What's brought this on? Why are you telling me now?"

"Because you catch killers, and I don't want you focusing on me and wasting your time or anyone else's. Promise me, Max, that you'll get those responsible. Promise me."

"I promise. This will be over soon, and you can rest assured that I won't discuss your relationship with anyone. Maybe you could tell Bonnie yourself when the time is right, but that's your business. Maybe Del was ready for a change in his life. Maybe he did want to dial back on work and make a go of things with you, but it's not my place to speak for him. All I know is that he must have been a wonderful man."

"Thank you so much. I'm sorry to come here and cry like this, as I'm sure you have better things to do than listen to me, but I'm glad I came."

"So am I, Veronica, and I'm truly sorry for your loss."

"No, don't be. Del was a kind, compassionate man and I'm proud to have been the one he chose to spend time with after being alone for so long. He deserved better, Max. "

Veronica stroked Anxious who had rested his head on her lap, along with the rest of his body, then lifted him down and stood. With a smile and a nod, she left then drove off, leaving me with more to think about.

But there was no time, and although a testament to Del's kindness as a man, and private nature as someone who would always be in the spotlight of his community, it wasn't relevant to what was about to happen.

I gave Anxious an early dinner as I wasn't sure how long what came next would take, then I sank into my chair and tried to put the pieces of this peculiar puzzle together. There was much that would have to wait a while, but I tried my best to get things as straight in my head as I could so I would be properly prepared for the approach I'd take to sort out this mess and get the case closed without causing more upset than was necessary.

With my legs stretched out, the grass tickling my toes, I settled back and waited.

It didn't take long.

Chapter 17

A gentle breeze swept across the airfield, warm, scented, and with a promise of a beautiful summer to come. I smiled as my hair blew into my face and my beard tickled my neck. Time for a facial hair trim, possibly even a haircut.

Anxious shifted at my feet with a groan, then curled up, head tucked in tight to his belly, about as content as any dog had ever been.

The plastic of the cheap camping chair dug into my back a little so I wiggled about, chuckling quietly to myself as I was just like my best buddy, although not as flexible. I'd grown to love this rather awkward, not quite natural way of sitting, and although I knew I could swap out the chair, it had done me so well ever since this wild ride began that it was now as much a part of my life as Vee.

With two sides of the gazebo zipped up, I was sheltered from most of the weather, but still had a great view out across the flat, manmade landscape so I could see the other residents and watch everyone coming and going. I loved days like this, sights like this, and although I hadn't met hardly anyone here I still felt close to them, like part of the community, as for all our differences we had so much in common.

Unable to help myself, and once again wondering why it brought me the absolute joy it did, I turned and surveyed my outdoor kitchen setup. The long, black-topped folding table along one wall at a right angle to Vee with the gas cooker, the chopping board, and the container for my cutlery and utensils there for when I needed it, the boxes stacked underneath containing crockery and cloths, another full of tins and random snacks, and a bright orange washing-up bowl. For some reason, the bowl was the one item I seemed to need to replace the most. Maybe I should try one of those collapsible ones instead so it could be packed flat rather than always being put in last and getting damaged? Something to look into, as like with everything else to do with vanlife, there were no end of options, from budget-friendly to eye-wateringly expensive.

The door to Vee was open, and the interior made me smile as it had ever since I first set eyes on this ancient relic of a van, still glorious after so many years. Sighing, I turned back to face the airfield and watched as several vehicles approached. My heart beat fast, I got a nervous knot in my stomach, and my skin prickled with the heat my body generated because of the nerves. It was crunch time, and I wasn't looking forward to it one bit.

"Looks like we've got guests, Anxious," I said softly, not really wanting to disturb him.

His ears pricked up and he grumbled, then he sniffed and released a short, sharp bark of excitement before standing and stretching out, ready for playtime as he clearly knew who was coming.

I got up and exited the gazebo and stood next to the trembling pooch, hardly able to contain himself and shaking worse than me now.

"You really like them, don't you?"

Anxious ran several circuits around me; I had my answer.

Moments later, the cars pulled to a stop and once it was safe to do so, Anxious tore off then skidded to a halt as he was undecided about his next course of action. Get admired by Melody first, try the old paw trick with Bonnie and hopefully get a treat or at least a cuddle, or launch at the twins and get double the fuss and plenty of nerve-jangling squealing? He chose the latter. With his head held high, his tail wagging so fast he might actually need the runway to get airborne, he barked a greeting then skipped over to the already excited twins then sat, tail swishing the grass, and lifted a paw in greeting.

Bonnie emerged from the driver's side and laughed. "Looks like Anxious is keen to play."

"He sure is. If he's not sleeping or eating, then he wants to have fun. Not that those things aren't fun too," I said with a smile.

"What about me?" asked Melody with a mock pout before she nodded and said, "Hey, Max."

"Hey. Everything okay? No problems?"

"Why would there be?" asked Bonnie, looking from me to Melody.

"No reason. Just a turn of phrase," said Melody, glancing at me.

"How are the girls?" I asked.

"As you can see, they're doing much better. I've been trying to keep them busy, and they're rather pleased they didn't go to school today as both of them were so upset last night and this morning. Neither slept well, not that I did either. They kept talking about Dad and how much they loved him, and it's been so awful. Sorry, I'm probably repeating myself. I know we saw you this morning, and sorry again for calling on you so early." Bonnie sniffled, then rubbed away her tears, but she was coping, and holding it together for her children.

"Can we take Anxious for a walk?" shouted Jane, or was it Kim? It was hard to tell from a distance.

"I don't think there's any choice now you said the W word," I laughed.

"Does he need his lead?" asked the other child.

"I'd take it with you, but he probably won't need it. Just be sure to call him back if he runs off too far, but I'm sure Anxious will be on his best behaviour." To make my point, I patted my pocket as my eyes met those of the hungriest dog in Wales. He gulped and showed he understood by licking his lips.

The girls came over with a very excited Anxious, so I got his lead then told them, "Don't let him go too far, and be sure to pick up his poo if he does one."

"Ugh, gross," said Kim.

"You have to," I insisted, handing them several poo bags. "People are walking around here, and nobody wants to stand in it. It's part of the responsibility of living with a dog."

"I'll do it," said Jane, taking the bags from me with a cheery smile.

"No, I want to," demanded Kim, trying to take the bags.

Bonnie smiled at her daughters, then told me, "If one wants to do something, so does the other."

"Hey, I have an idea," I said. "Why not take one bag each? Whoever gets there first can clear up after Anxious. Deal?"

"Deal!"

The girls skipped off, holding hands, already talking quietly to each other as Anxious ran off ahead then kept racing back to see why they were being so slow.

Turning to Bonnie, I asked, "I hope that's okay?"

"Of course. Trust me, it will not be a long walk. They'll be back in five minutes complaining about being tired and demanding snacks."

"Anxious will want the snacks, but he could run around all day, and often does. Shall we sit, or would you rather stand? Would you like a drink? I have tea, coffee, or wine if you'd prefer?"

"Max, I would absolutely adore a glass of wine." Bonnie's hair blew into her face and when she parted it her eyes were brimming with tears.

"Hey, it's alright. This will be over soon."

"It will? How can you be so sure? How do you know? This is like a nightmare."

"You have to trust Max," said Melody, putting an arm around Bonnie, her eyes meeting mine, her face grim.

"I do trust you, Max, but I hardly know you. You've spent all your time trying to figure this thing out, but even the detectives have no idea what happened. I spoke to them earlier and they're still scratching their heads. It's so ridiculous. How could Dad have known he was going to be murdered? How did he know you were going to come? It's a twisted, sick joke. The killer will never be found."

"Or killers," I reminded her. "Let me fix you that drink. Melody, what would you like?"

"I'll take a glass of wine too."

I nodded, then went to fix the drinks, deciding Prosecco wasn't the best choice as it would seem like we were celebrating, and we most definitely were not. Instead, I chose the only other bottle in the fridge, a basic Pinot, but a nice one, and set three glasses out on the little coffee table then squatted while I poured the drinks.

Bonnie took hers with shaking hands and nodded her thanks, then sipped. I handed Melody hers then retrieved mine, and together we drank in silence, watching the girls skip around with a barking Anxious, the three having a great time, all worries forgotten for a little while. I lamented what the future held, but at least they were having fun now. It would be tough for the family, but for the twins in particular it would be a very rough time ahead and their lives changed forever because of Del's death.

"To Del," I said, raising my glass.

"To Del," said Melody.

"Miss you, Dad," choked Bonnie.

We drank as we watched the girls slowly make their way back to us, so I knew it was now or never to warn Bonnie that things were about to get a whole lot worse before they got better. I almost choked on my words, so took another drink, then a very deep breath, looked at Bonnie who nodded sadly, then set my glass down.

"Max, is everything alright? Thank you for inviting us. We needed a break from the fuss at home. People mean well, but they keep knocking the door or calling and I can't handle another condolence. It's kind of them, but it's too much."

"I'm afraid I had an ulterior motive," I admitted. "You aren't going to like this, but I felt it was best that it was just us when I explained. No need to involve the police yet."

"I don't understand. What do you mean? I appreciate you both trying to solve this, but don't feel bad for being unable to get to the truth. I wish you had, but it's okay."

"No, that's not it at all," said Melody, smiling softly, full of sympathy. "It's the opposite. Max figured it out. He picks up on these little things, the clues, I guess, and somehow puts the pieces together. We're so sorry, Bonnie, but it's time to come clean."

"You mean me? You want me to admit it?" she asked, shocked, and sipping her wine nervously. "I would never. Could never. He was my dad and I loved him."

"We know you did, and we know it wasn't you, Bonnie," I explained.

"Then who was it? What is this? If you've got something to say, then please say it. I can't stand this. It's too much. I'm heartbroken." She paused to rub rather forcibly at her already red eyes, then blurted, inconsolable, "He's gone forever and I don't know what to do. Am I losing my mind? What are you saying? Out with it!"

"It's not an easy thing to tell you. In fact, it's the hardest thing I've ever done," I admitted, wiping my eyes, forcing down the sadness I felt.

"Just tell me, Max. If you know, then I demand to be told. Who killed my father?"

I turned away and watched the twins approach, laughing as they skipped along, hand in hand, Anxious panting beside them, behaving impeccably as he got closer as he knew he'd be rewarded for good behaviour.

Melody watched them, too, tears running down her cheeks.

Bonnie picked up on the tense atmosphere and gasped, "You can't be serious? My girls? You don't mean it was them, surely? What is happening here?"

"I think the best thing is if we let the children explain. I don't want to say anything to make things worse."

"Max, this is not funny. Are you really saying my sweet, innocent children murdered their grandfather? Their Grampy? Of course they wouldn't. They'd never hurt a fly."

"And I agree. Like I said, it's complicated, and please prepare yourself for what will happen. This will be an upsetting time for your family, but I didn't know how else to handle this."

"Neither did I," said Melody. "I'm so sorry, Bonnie, truly I am. We thought this was for the best. Away from everyone else, no distractions, and to ensure the girls are safe and don't do anything foolish like run off."

"Why would they run off?" she snapped, whirling on me and jabbing her finger. "You! What have you done? What nonsense is this? You better explain yourself. Right now!"

"Mum, what's going on?" asked Jane as she clutched her sister's hand tight and sucked on a strand of hair, eyes darting from her mother to me then Melody.

"Nothing, dear. Did you have a nice walk?"

"The best! Anxious is so cool. Can we get a dog? Can we? Please?"

"Yes, please, Mum?" whined Kim, smiling at Bonnie. "We'll take him for walks every day and even clean up the poo. Not that we had to today, which is a relief. Can we get a dog?"

"We'll see. Maybe we will."

The girls cheered, sending Anxious into an excited frenzy, so I gave him a few biscuits so he'd calm and he took them over to the groundsheet and settled in the shade of the gazebo for his snack.

While the girls chatted excitedly about the possibility of having a new best friend, us adults said nothing, the atmosphere tense, waiting to boil over. Bonnie was a wreck already, not knowing what to think or what on earth this was really about. She was about to speak when I held up a hand and nodded that I would explain what I'd uncovered, so she nodded back.

We faced the happy twins and I said, "Girls, I'm afraid there's some news about your grandfather."

"What news?" asked Kim.

"You know Melody and I have been trying to figure out what on earth could have happened?" They nodded as they glanced at each other, then their heads lowered. "You know about the note he left and how confusing it was? That everyone was searching for a man or woman who had killed him in the most terrible of ways?"

"It was awful. Everyone said so. Poor Grampy." Jane was already crying, and it broke my heart, but I had to continue. Bonnie stepped between the girls and put an arm around each of them, leaving Melody and I to face the three distraught family members.

"It really was, and everyone's been trying their very best to figure things out and bring the killer to justice. You understand what I'm saying?"

The twins nodded, mute, heads down.

"Max, please don't do this," sobbed Bonnie. "There must be a mistake. Something isn't right here. It can't be true."

"Bonnie, it's okay. It isn't what you think. Don't be afraid." Melody stepped forward and lifted the chins of each twin gently until they focused on her. "You heard that? Don't be afraid, but it is time for the truth. You have to tell the truth." Melody stepped back and smiled in sympathy at me, knowing how hard this was for me as well as the family.

It was incredibly tough for her too. She'd held it together and brought the family here, yet we'd agreed this was for the best and would allow us to talk without fear of interruption or anything getting out of hand if things didn't go as planned.

Another deep breath, then I continued. "Girls, we're on your side here. We want to let Del rest in peace, and he'd hate for people to be spending time hunting for a killer if the police, and us, could be doing other things. There are really bad people the detectives could be catching, but right now they're spending their time looking into this. It has to end. So, I want you to tell us everything."

"Go on, you can do it," encouraged Melody.

"Nobody is judging, nobody will shout, or tell you off. We just need to know. Does that make sense?"

"Yes," they whispered.

"Then let's start with the most obvious thing, so you can relax a little and know that we aren't going to blame you. Your mum is beside herself with worry, so she deserves the truth, doesn't she?"

"We're sorry," they chorused.

"It was an accident, wasn't it? A game gone horribly wrong? Don't be afraid, but you must be honest. Del would want that."

"We didn't mean to do it," blurted Kim, rubbing at her red eyes, gripping her sister tight then flinging herself at a startled Bonnie.

She clutched first one daughter, then both, tight, looking at me over their shoulders as they sobbed in her arms. She was clearly confused, and very shocked, but I hoped that in a few minutes everything would be cleared up and she could have closure on what had been the most confusing murder mystery I'd ever been involved in. Especially because, as it turned out, no murder had even been committed.

Chapter 18

"Of course you didn't," I said, hoping I sounded non-confrontational. "Can you tell us what did happen? You know we've all been very confused by it, and your poor mother deserves an explanation, don't you think?"

"We're so sorry," sobbed Kim.

Bonnie released her children and held them at arm's length, then said, "Whatever it is, you can tell us. I will always love you, no matter what, and I know you would never hurt Grampy on purpose. You'll feel better once you explain."

"We've felt so awful," mumbled Jane. "Kim and me didn't know what to do and we hated lying, but we thought we'd be in so much trouble."

"We're going to go to jail now. We'll get picked on by the big girls and they'll beat us up and we'll turn into awful criminals and never get out!"

"That won't happen," I insisted, hating to see them like this, knowing there was no other choice. "First, can I confirm that you already knew about me? That you've been watching videos and going on forums where they discuss the cases I've been involved in?"

"We think you're so cool," said Kim, blushing despite the circumstances.

"Everyone thinks so. There's a forum where we chat about your mysteries and all the girls think you're amazing."

"That's nice," I said, wishing nobody had ever heard of me. "So you showed Del some of the videos? You watched vanlife stuff with him?"

"For a few weeks now. Once we got into it, it looked so cool and even Grampy was interested. He said it would be a great idea and that we should go on a trip together. Maybe in the summer holidays. Mum, we were going to surprise you. Grampy was going to buy a van and we were going to help him convert it. We could go tour around Europe for the summer and he could visit his suppliers, but we could all go. It would have been so much fun."

"I don't know if that would have ever happened, but it's nice you had an interest together. But how does this relate to Grampy's death? I still don't understand."

Jane took a step away, lifted her head, and admitted, "It was just a game. It went horribly wrong and we didn't know what to do. It's all ruined and now he's dead and we'll never go on our trip and we're going to jail forever. What about school? We won't get to go to university or ever get a job and we'll die in prison!"

"That won't happen. They don't do that to children, and besides, you didn't kill him, did you?"

"We didn't touch him," said Kim, joining her sister and taking her hand. "We were playing, and it went wrong. All Grampy wanted to do was have fun with us and he wasn't really that interested in vanlife. He was just saying that to make us happy."

"He liked it a bit, but not like us. He said it was one of our fads and we'd grow out of it, but we insisted it wasn't and we would do it for real when we grew up. He agreed to watch the videos and learn about Max because he did so much cool stuff, and he got really interested. Like, for real. It was awesome."

"He really did think it was fun," agreed Jane. "We were so pleased, and talked about it loads when we went over to visit."

"So that's why you've been going over so much the last few weeks, especially after school?" asked Bonnie. "So you could watch videos and follow Max around online? I assume people talk about where he's going and wonder what he'll be doing next?"

"Yes, exactly," said Kim, gasping for air, her face brightening a little, most probably because nobody had told them off yet or insisted they'd be going to jail.

"Now we come to the morning that Del died." I smiled at the girls, nodding encouragement, and what little confidence and hope they had vanished.

They burst into tears and hugged their mother, and it simply got worse. What began as quiet crying became wracking sobs, so forceful I thought they would be sick. Their faces were bright red and blotchy, tiny fists clenched, but Anxious knew what to do and pawed at their legs gently but insistently until they took notice.

"He wants to help, and he wants this to be over. Give him a fuss as he hates seeing his friends upset, then just tell us what happened and it will be over. Trust me, nothing will be as bad as this."

"But we'll have to go to the police station," whined Jane, rubbing at her eyes then wiping her sister's before they both squatted to console Anxious.

"Yes, you will, but your mum will be there and the officers will understand. Be brave, be braver than you've ever been in your lives, and just come out with it. A few minutes, that's all, then you'll be free of the burden. Does that sound okay?"

"Okay. We'll do it!" Jane nodded to her sister and she did the same, then they stood before us and out it came in one long breath from Jane. "We'd played a silly game the night before. That Grampy had died and Max was the one who found him and uncovered the killer. We did it in the living room. Grampy lay on the floor after pretending to be stabbed, and I played Max and Kim played Min. We used a teddy to be Anxious and we had so much fun."

"Girls, that was in terrible taste," chastised Bonnie.

"It was only a game, and he enjoyed it. Anyway, we came home, you remember, Mum, and we were hyped and really happy?"

"I remember. You couldn't settle and took an age to get to sleep."

"We know. But in the morning, Grampy texted me, and said he had a big surprise for us. You said we could go out to play early as we had the day off school because of the burst pipes, so we hurried over to see Grampy. The door was unlocked so we crept in, whispering and giggling, and then we heard him call to us from the back."

"So you went to find him?" asked Melody.

"I went first," said Kim.

"You did, but I was right behind you. Grampy was in the kitchen and writing something. He showed it to us, and it was the note to you, Max. We thought it was hilarious, especially the soggy bottom."

"But Grampy was genuinely upset about that part. He hated that the quiche wasn't perfect."

"Hey, I'm telling the story!" complained Jane. "He said he had an even better idea for our game, as he'd been following the forums and people had reported seeing you coming right down the street. He knew you loved food, so thought you might stop by. We were going to surprise you with some free food and tell you we were your greatest fans. He was so excited as he knew we loved the mysteries you got involved in."

"So he did know I was coming? I was spotted and someone posted it straight away?"

"Yes, and we couldn't wait to meet you. We decided to play our game again, so he wrote that note to you then we followed him into the office and he put it in an envelope. Then we went back into the kitchen and he wrote another one and gave it to us. When we read it, we couldn't wait to get started."

"What did the note say, girls?" asked Bonnie, white with shock, her hands trembling, but smiling at the girls so as not to scare them.

"Here it is. We kept it, as we didn't know what else to do. Everything went so wrong." Jane pulled out a slip of paper from her denim jacket pocket and handed it to Bonnie.

Bonnie took a moment to read it, then shook her head. "I… I can't read it out loud. Max, will you?" She handed it to me and I nodded.

"Jane and Kim, the best detectives in the country, please come and find my killer. I'm out the back and there's been a terrible murder. Hurry. Maybe get Max to help you when he arrives. But be careful. Lots of love, Grampy. X."

"We couldn't stop laughing. We'd already played the game, but this was different as while we were reading it Grampy got one of his really sharp knives, the one he said about in your note, Max, and held it up, pretending to look scared."

"That was very irresponsible. He should know better than to play with knives." Bonnie shook her head, unable to accept what her father had done.

"Mum, it was just make-believe. He was careful with it, but then he hurried out to the back door and we followed behind, giggling. He… he slipped on the step as he jumped down into the lane, and it got confusing then. He kind of twisted, or something, we aren't sure, and fell against the wall with the knife held up. He was just standing there with it in his throat, then he smiled at us before he fell over. He was dead. We screamed, but then we freaked out. We locked the door and ran away and raced back home to hide in our room. We didn't know what to do and knew everyone would be so upset and angry with us. Are you? Do you hate us? Is it our fault? It is, isn't it? We killed Grampy because we made him play that dumb game and now he's gone forever."

"You aren't to blame," I said. "It was a terrible accident and nothing more. A game, like you said, and that's all it was. Your Grampy was a great man from what I've heard, and he wouldn't want you to feel responsible. He fell, and that's it. I'm so sorry, girls, but you have to know that it wasn't anything you did."

"Max is right, girls. A game gone wrong. I know this is upsetting for you both, but you told the truth and that's all that matters."

"But we ran away!" Jane stepped away from the others, gnawing at her knuckles, and stamped her foot. "We left him there. Dead in the alley by the bins. We loved him so much and we left him. Like he was a bag of stinking rubbish."

"It's… You…" Bonnie couldn't speak, so I stepped forward.

"You're looking at it all wrong. I know you feel guilty, and maybe you should, just a little, but see it from his point of view. Del, your Grampy, died doing what he loved even more than running his shop. He died playing with the two favourite women in his life. You two. He shouldn't have been playing with a knife, and that isn't your fault, but he was happy, and that's what matters. You said it yourself, that right before he died he smiled at you. Always remember the happy times you had with him, never the one bad thing. Don't feel guilty. I know you won't accept that yet, but when you're older, you will. You are young children and young children wouldn't know how to deal with what happened. You did the right thing and told us, so don't feel bad."

"Max is right, girls," said Melody. "Del wouldn't want you to take this burden on yourselves. The silly sod played with a very dangerous knife and had an accident. Terrible, but that's all."

"You're sure?" sniffled Kim. "But we didn't tell anyone, and we let Mum find out from the police. That makes us bad."

"It doesn't make you bad," I said. "It makes you just what you are. Young girls. Death can be scary, and adults would have panicked just like you did. You're good girls, that's obvious."

Bonnie was trying to regain her composure for the girls' sake, but it was a lot for her to handle. Finally, she found her voice and spoke. "You should have told me straight away, but I understand why you didn't. You were frightened and in shock. You might not understand, but when bad things happen, your brain does funny things and kind of shuts down. You do things you would never normally do. Sometimes people even forget entirely. You aren't to blame. I can't believe it, but this really was just an unfortunate accident with some strange coincidences."

"Really?" asked Kim.

"Yes, really. And I bet Grampy is watching us right now and grumbling about his soggy bottom."

"He did hate a soggy bottom," sniggered Kim.

I think the fact we all laughed then surprised us, but death does have a funny way of doing things to your head. Bonnie was right about that.

The laughter was short-lived and it left us feeling rather guilty. The girls asked what would happen next and Bonnie explained that in a short while they would go to the police station and ask for the detectives, then they would have to tell the story again.

It was upsetting for them but they understood, and were clearly relieved that they weren't in as much trouble as they'd believed. Bonnie suggested they take Anxious for another walk, which they agreed to in a heartbeat, and raced off, pleased to get away from us, as no matter how much we tried to hide it, it was clear we were rather shocked by the truth.

Once they were across the airfield, Bonnie said, "I had to get them away so I can think. Max, and you, Melody, thank you so much for handling that so well. I don't think I could have kept my cool otherwise."

"I hope we did the right thing getting them to explain like this," I said, still unsure.

"You handled it better than I would have if I'd found out any other way. It must have been eating the poor things up inside. Is it true? The note to you, the crazy way they said he died? Someone posted about it and they wanted to play a game then give you some treats if you came into the shop?"

"I think it's all true, yes. One of those crazy coincidences. Of course, he never meant for me to read the note. He wrote it to entertain the girls. It went wrong and we believed it meant something it didn't. We've been looking in the wrong places all this time, when the truth was right in front of us."

"I can't even image how you figured this out, but thank you."

"After how kind you've been to me, it was the least I could do. I'm sorry this isn't just over now, but at least some of the guilt has been lifted from the girls."

"Yes, but it's going to take them a good while to get over this. I'm so relieved we know now, but in a way I wish he had been murdered."

"So the twins wouldn't have been involved?" asked Melody.

"Yes. But I know my girls, and it will fade, and I'll ensure that I always remind them that they did nothing wrong. They should have told me, but they're young children and got scared. I forgive them, and I forgive Dad for being such an idiot and playing with a knife in front of them. Oh, Dad, why did you have to be so silly?"

"Then you will be fine." I did something I never usually did and hugged Bonnie. She almost collapsed into my arms, and remained there, crying softly, until we heard the girls returning.

She wiped her eyes, brushed back her hair, and plastered on a strained smile when they got close, putting on a brave face like I knew she always would when they needed her.

"It's time to go," she told them.

The mood turned sombre as they piled into the car, leaving Melody, Anxious, and I watching them go.

Chapter 19

I hung around for a few weeks while funeral arrangements were made, the will was sorted out, and the endless paperwork completed. It was a very straightforward affair with Bonnie .business, and a generous cash gift for Melody; a welcome shock for her but she was beyond grateful that Del had thought of her so highly.

The entire town was shocked by Del's passing, but nobody ever learned the truth of what really happened. The kind detectives put it down to accidental death by misadventure, which was the truth, and no word of the twins' involvement ever reached the ears of the likes of Sam from the newsagents, Constance, Del's rival, or Charlie the milkman. The once seemingly impossible to understand note was kept on file with the rest of the paperwork from Del's case, explained away as merely a joke from a man who had become rather obsessed with vanlife and one person in particular. Me!

Over the weeks, the girls began to accept that they truly had done nothing wrong beyond getting scared and running off when they should have told their mum, and they mourned Del's passing in the proper manner, with plenty of cuddles from Bonnie. They also spent an inordinate amount of time with me at the airfield, and both Bonnie and Melody enjoyed the escape from the sad business of dealing with Del's affairs.

We became quite close, and I filled everyone in on everything I'd learned about vanlife, both the good and the not so good, and they were eager to learn as much as I could think of to tell. The twins became somewhat of a permanent fixture at the site, getting to know all the more long-term residents, and always eager to greet new arrivals and explain how things worked at my temporary home in Wales. It became quite the little community, in no small part thanks to the two innocents who skipped around the massive site, hand in hand, giggling and chatting away to often rather bemused people who'd come for some peace and quiet.

Anxious was in his element, overjoyed to have company more his own age for a change, the girls' childlike wonder and seemingly never dwindling energy meaning he ended each day exhausted and happy after racing around with them and playing hide and seek until it was time for them to go. I often split the duty of ferrying the girls back and forth between Bonnie or Melody, but we spent many evenings together sitting in the camping chairs, chatting, eating, and watching the twins run around with Anxious' ears bouncing as he barked when he found one of them hiding and won the game.

As it inevitably does, days passed and then it was weeks later and most things to do with Del's affairs were sorted. I'd done what I could to help, but Bonnie handled things well with plenty of support from her husband, but mostly it was Melody who helped Bonnie keep it together and deal with a seemingly endless number of suppliers and business arrangements that had to be updated now Del was no longer in charge. Bonnie decided to keep the business, and run it just as it always had been, and she kept the name Del's Deli out of respect for her father and to honour his memory.

What surprised me, and definitely Melody, was that Bonnie took the unusual step of splitting the entire business fifty fifty with Melody, making them joint partners. Plus, Melody got to move into the flat above the shop. She rented out her own house so had the income from that to supplement the generous wage from the deli where she and Melody decided they would both work. Melody kept her full-time hours, Bonnie worked around the children and the endless chores involved in running a household, and the girls would help out on Saturdays like they always had.

It all began to come together slowly over the weeks, with plenty of tears and reminiscing whilst everyone gradually came to terms with what had happened. I did what I could, helped when asked or I felt it was needed, but mostly kept my assistance to matters concerning the deli and the mammoth food operation Del undertook every morning. Melody couldn't manage it alone, and certainly had no interest in getting up at four every morning, but I showed her how to streamline the operation and how best to prepare the daily offerings, and as it turned out it wasn't Melody but Bonnie who took over the early morning routine of preparing the mouthwatering offerings while her husband did the school run.

Things slowly began to slot into place, and the beginnings of new routines formed, but I could tell that it was still too soon for Bonnie to handle it without first getting some time for herself and the girls away from so many memories. Del's presence was still everywhere they looked, and she often broke down in the shop or while in the middle of a conversation, but Melody always calmed her and the two became very close and best friends.

Del's funeral was a massive affair with the service at the church so busy they actually set up speakers outside so those who couldn't fit inside could hear the beautiful eulogy from the vicar and the heart-wrenching speech Bonnie gave that ended with a round of applause. The wake was held at a local club that again was filled beyond capacity with as many people outside as in, and I found myself with Bonnie, Melody, and the twins off to one side in a beautiful courtyard to get some space from the constant stream of people offering their condolences. Tony mingled, thanking the numerous mourners for coming, holding them at bay for a few precious minutes.

Bonnie was exhausted, but I could tell that this was the closure she and the girls needed, who both looked very pretty in their plain but elegant dark dresses, their stunning long blond hair shining in the March sunshine. Their slender bare arms reminded me how young and delicate they still were, which was easy to forget at times as one minute they seemed so grown up, the next the young children they actually were.

"Do you need to go home?" I asked Bonnie. "You're worn out. This has been a long day and I don't think anyone would mind. Not that it matters if they did. You did your father proud."

"We are going to head off in a little while. Max, thank you for all you've done. I know you have things to do and places to go, so we truly appreciate you staying to help. You've been a lifesaver."

"You really have," agreed Melody, looking just as exhausted. "I would never have managed at the shop without you. Or you, Bonnie."

"It was nothing, and you both have everything under control. Bonnie, you're a natural born cook, and Del would be proud."

"And not even a soggy bottom," teased Melody kindly, smiling warmly at Bonnie.

"No soggy bottoms on my watch," laughed Bonnie, tucking a stray strand of hair behind her ear, trying, but failing, to hide her tiredness and how sad she was.

"I'm glad I hung around," I said. "It's been inspiring seeing how well you both coped, and now the shop is open again I think it's exactly how Del would have wanted it to be. You'll make an unstoppable team."

"We really will. It's been good for me, and for the girls, to have the shop to keep us busy. Although, I'm glad the paperwork is mostly finished. Just a few more things to sort out, then everything will be official."

"And I'm going to move into the flat in a few days. I can't wait. It's bigger than my entire house, and it means I can just get up and I'm already at work. Bonnie, are you sure about me having half the business?"

"Absolutely! You deserve it, and Del would be so happy. I know he only left the shop to me as he wouldn't want to hurt my feelings, but this is right, and he'd be pleased with the decision."

"I think it's the perfect solution. You work so well together. But you do need a break from everything," I told Bonnie. "You too, Melody."

"Funny you should say that." Bonnie winked at Melody, and they both grinned, then the girls began to giggle.

"What's so funny?" I looked from one smiling face to the next, then all four burst out laughing.

"Can I tell him?" asked Jane.

"No, let me," demanded Kim, the girls hopping from one foot to the other, causing Anxious to get excited and his ears prick up, waiting for his new best friends to start counting so he could go and hide.

I calmed him down with a well-deserved biscuit while the others argued good-naturedly about who could tell me whatever the news was. Once he settled, I asked, "What is it?"

"We're vanlifers now," blurted Kim.

"Just like you, Max," agreed Jane.

"What's this?" I asked Bonnie.

"Melody and I discussed it, and what we decided is that the shop will close for a month while we make some changes, give the place a facelift, a lick of paint, re-arrange the interior, and Melody can decorate the flat."

"I'm going to get some help, but I'll be living there so I can do the painting and handle the workmen."

"Um, that's great. Excellent idea. Now is probably the best time to do it. So that's the news? That doesn't make you vanlifers," I told the twins.

"No, silly, not that. We are vanlifers, aren't we?" Kim asked Bonnie.

"Yes, sort of. Not like Max, as it isn't permanent, but we've just bought a VW Transporter and me and the girls are going away for a month to travel around the country and have a lovely break. Their dad can't come because of work, but he's going to track us down every weekend and stay with us then."

"That's a great idea." I high-fived the girls and kissed Bonnie's cheek, all of them beaming. "You'll have a wild time. You deserve it. All of you do."

The girls ran off with Anxious, seemingly having got a second wind now they'd told me the news. We watched them go, then I asked Bonnie, "How are they doing?"

"Not too bad at all. They're coping, and have accepted it wasn't their fault. That Del just had an accident and they weren't to blame. They're coming to terms with things slowly."

"That's good news. They're lovely girls. The break will do them wonders. You too."

"It will. I discussed it with the school, and as long as I do school work every day with them, they're fine about it. They were very understanding."

"And when they get back, we'll have a grand re-opening, and figure out our new routine properly," said Melody.

"That's perfect. It will give you a fresh start, and I think Del would be so proud of you all. He'd want the girls to have this trip, especially as he was so into it like they are. Have fun, enjoy the time with them, but I know you'll miss the shop and it will be strange being away from home."

"It will, but a change is what we need. It's only a month, but it will do us good. A little space from the madness. Max, thank you once again for everything you've done, and what do you think is next for you and Anxious?"

"I honestly haven't thought about it. I'll see where we end up, and wherever that may be, I'm sure it will be perfect. That's the beauty of my life. Every day is different, but some things are always the same. I'm glad I could be of help these past few weeks, but I'm so sorry you had to deal with any of it."

"At least we can move on with our lives now, and that's down to you. It breaks my heart to know the girls had to go through this, but it would have been much worse if you didn't get them to tell the truth. Plus, it was driving me mad not knowing. I couldn't have handled that for much longer."

"Now it's over with and we've got a great future ahead of us." Melody smiled at Bonnie and their closeness was apparent. The two hugged, then pulled me in for a cuddle too.

When we broke, I called for Anxious, who came bombing back with the twins in tow, so we said our goodbyes then left. After the last few weeks, I felt in need of a break, too, and some personal space to recharge my batteries.

The drive back to the airfield was gloriously quiet, and this chapter of my life was finally behind me. Once parked beside the gazebo, I smiled as I settled into my chair, slipped off my Crocs, and watched as Anxious curled up with a sigh then began to snore. It felt like coming home, and I sat, enjoying the solitude, grateful for everything I had in my life, but missing Min dreadfully.

The late afternoon stretched out before me, and after a cuppa, I dozed, then continued to sit in peace, a man and his dog, both happy, not wanting for anything we didn't already have. I watched my neighbours come and go but remained seated, just watching the world go by, content with my lot like I don't think I had ever been until now. After the whirlwind of the last few weeks, and the intense emotions around me, I needed this time to gather myself and get centred; I never wanted it to end.

Afternoon turned to evening, and yet I was still loathe to move, happy that nobody came calling, and I was left alone with my exhausted best buddy who continued to sleep.

Then inspiration hit and I came up with a cunning plan for my dinner. A quiche with a twist, cooked in my large cast-iron pot, so I set about building a small fire in the fire bowl and then once again resumed my sitting marathon and watched the flames dance brightly, licking the edge of the bowl, sparks shooting towards the sky like miniature fireworks.

I could have stayed there all night, but I had kitchen prep to do, so I heaved out of my trusty chair and hummed to myself happily while I got busy in my kitchen making pastry, slicing onions, grating cheese, beating eggs, and generally having a great time.

Several hours later, as I truly was in no hurry and the pastry always cooked better if left for a while before it was baked, I settled down with a huge slice of perfectly cooked quiche, buttery boiled potatoes, and a salad, and ate. A frosty glass of wine helped wash down a perfect meal. Then I cleaned up, sorted out a few things, hung up my tea towel and washcloth, then enjoyed the rest of the evening alone.

I'd loved having Bonnie, the twins, and Melody come almost every evening, but spending time with Anxious where it was just us was beautiful, and having him curled up on my lap was what I needed to finally put Del's death behind me and stop worrying about the twins. I never normally got close to the people I met when death was involved, but this time it had been very different, and much more personal, and I'd truly wanted to stick around to help in any way I could. It turned out to have been good for us all, but boy was I glad it was over.

By the time it was dark, I felt fully recovered, and ready for another adventure, but that could wait until tomorrow, as I intended to do nothing else but sit. The sky was clear, a black blanket with trillions of pinpricks of light, and warm enough that I stayed in my shorts beside the fire. Adding the occasional log or pouring a glass of wine were my only movements besides stroking Anxious, and there we remained long into the night, mesmerised by the flames, content in each other's company.

When it was finally time for bed, I groaned, as for the first time in many months I'd forgotten to sort out the rock n roll bed, so got busy with that, readied for sleep, then crawled in and cuddled up to Anxious who lay on the pillow beside me. As my head hit the tiny space he'd left me, he opened an eye, grinned, then licked my nose.

"Goodnight, Anxious. Sleep well. Tomorrow is another day and another chance for an adventure. I wonder what we'll do?"

Anxious snored, and I smiled.

The End

But not quite. Stick around and flip to the next page for a stunning one-pot recipe and for a little about the next book in the series.

Recipe

Nanny Beryl's Cheese & Tomato Quiche

Some form of oven is needed for this, a Dutch Oven with a rimmed lid so it can hold coals being the perfect option if you want to use a fire, but you might want to raise it up on a trivet or rack of some sort. Of course you can use a conventional appliance if cooking at home, or you're one of those fancy people with all the mod-cons in your home on wheels!

Quiche is one of those dishes that is a true delight once mastered, and as long as you follow a few simple steps, you should end up with a perfectly cooked star with definitely no soggy bottom! If you want to be a stickler for the one-pot rule, then cook the quiche first then do your potatoes, or simply whip up a salad, or whatever takes your fancy. Alternatively, just enjoy the quiche. It's so moreish, that you'll want a few slices anyway, and it's a very filling and delicious treat all on its own, either hot or cold the next day.

This isn't a cream-laden, rich quiche, rather a simpler affair perfect for a picnic, warm or cold. If you have to, add some ham, or cooked bacon along with the mushrooms. Nanny Beryl was keen to keep it veggie, though, and frankly it really is rather good for it.

Ingredients

For the Pastry

- 250g plain flour
- 125g cold unsalted butter, cubed
- Pinch of salt
- Ice cold water (4-5 few tablespoons)

For the Filling

- 1 tin plum tomatoes, drained and squeezed as dry as possible
- 1/2 tsp dried oregano
- 1 onion, finely sliced
- 150g button mushrooms roughly chopped
- 5 eggs, whisked and seasoned
- 200g cheddar cheese grated
- Salt & ground black pepper

Method

You could cheat with shop-bought pastry but Nanny might not approve, so here's how she did it.

- First make the pastry. Rub together the flour and butter between your fingertips until it resembles fine breadcrumbs. Then add 4 tbsp of ice-cold water and mix to form a ball of dough. You might need a little more water, it should leave the bowl reasonably clean when the pastry is the right consistency. Wrap in clingfilm and refrigerate for at least 30 mins, but a few days won't hurt.
- When you're ready to put your quiche together preheat the oven 200°C/400°F/Gas Mark 6. On a flour dusted surface roll the pastry and line a well buttered flan tin (8 or 9 inch).
- Nanny would never do this bit, and hers was always wonderful, but for me blind baking is a must. First bake for 15 mins lined with baking parchment and baking beans. Remove the beans and parchment and bake for another 10 mins until just crisp and lightly coloured.

- Reduce the oven temperature to 180°C/350°F/Gas Mark 4.
- Time to assemble the quiche. Firstly line with the drained plum tomatoes (flatten them out to cover the base as evenly as possible). Grind over a generous amount of black pepper and the dried oregano.
- Then layer with the finely sliced onions and sprinkle with the chopped mushrooms.
- Cover the quiche with an even layer of cheese and then gently pour over the egg.
- On a baking tray, bake your quiche for 40-45 minutes until just set and golden.

This is great hot, cold, or warm, with salad, spuds, or nothing at all. It was the quiche of childhood birthday teas in the Rhodes' household, so most often eaten with potato salad, crisps, and cake!

Smacznego!

From the Author

I'm sure we've all learned not to play with knives, especially fancy Japanese Shapiro ones, but at least Del died doing what he loved the most in this world.

The more I research vanlife, and get sucked into the never-ending online world of YouTube and the number of people recording their experiences, the more I realise just how massive a movement it has become.

More people than ever before are taking holidays in the UK rather than travelling abroad, which is great, and the fact that so many choose to either camp in tents, or sleep in vehicles is testament to just how beautiful the country is, and the benefits of being close to nature.

As I write this, we have a week until Christmas and my son is beyond excited. The wind is howling, the rain is making a quagmire of my yard, but I can stare out of my office window and smile as the birds fill their tummies from the three feeders, and watch the last few leaves get blown from an ancient Sycamore that makes me work hard on the gutters of our shed for many months.

I wouldn't have it any other way, and yet my campervan is calling to me, reminding me that the warmer months are just around the corner and the shortest day is almost upon us. Not long now until warm summer days and long, light evenings, and just like Max I cannot wait to slip on my cut-offs, take off my socks, and parade around in a pair of Crocs. Although, and I know Max would disagree vehemently, I keep them strictly for wearing at home, never for in public.

Apart from at campsites, as that doesn't count, right? Right?

Time for book 13, and trust me, you're not going to want to miss this next adventure. Hold on tight, as things are about to get hair-raising. Death Slides and Cheese Pies might be an unusual name, but it'll make sense soon, I promise.

Be sure to stay updated about new releases and fan sales. You'll hear about them first. No spam, just book updates at www.authortylerrhodes.com.

You can also follow me on Amazon www.amazon.com/stores/author/B0BN6T2VQ5.

Connect with me on Facebook www.facebook.com/authortylerrhodes/